April, 2010

Wit

MW01098982

.

Lori's Quest

CHARLOTTE MILLER ENBERG

authorHOUSE™

1663 LIBERTY DRIVE, SUITE 200
BLOOMINGTON, INDIANA 47403
(800) 839-8640
WWW.AUTHORHOUSE.COM

This book is a work of fiction. People, places, events, and situations are the product of the author's imagination. Any resemblance to actual persons, living or dead, or historical events, is purely coincidental.

First published by AuthorHouse 1/24/2006

ISBN: 1-4259-0260-X (sc)

Printed in the United States of America
Bloomington, Indiana

This book is printed on acid-free paper.

This is a book about my childhood in the pioneer
days of British Columbia
Although the story itself is fictional, it accurately
depicts the conditions under which we lived, and the
struggle to adjust to our new country. .

This book is dedicated to the memory of my mother and
father
Jacob and Erna Schroeder

One

" Papa, are you certain I must enroll in my new school today?" Lori looked up at her father, her eyes pleading. With the cold gray building looming before her she felt, for the first time, a wave of fear. "It's already the end of February, and if we waited 'till fall I could get used to my new home and wouldn't feel so afraid."

"Of course you must begin today or you will not finish grade six. That is enough talk about it," answered her father. The girl followed him through the front door of the school up to the classroom marked "Grades Four to Eight", which he opened with a steady, resolute hand.

He walked towards the front of the room and spoke to the woman who had been instructing the children, all sitting in neat rows. "I would like to present to you my daughter, Elenore Mueller, who will be attending grade six. She comes from a school near Winnipeg, Manitoba." Lori noticed that her father spoke slowly and carefully, as though he had practiced and planned every word he would say. And although every word was correctly spoken, the German accent was very evident, even to her.

"I am Miss Kent," said the lady instructing the class. "I am very glad to meet you. However, since class is already in session I must ask you to return after school so that I can obtain the necessary information concerning Elenore. It is Mr.Mueller, isn't it?"

"Yes, it is," answered Mr. Mueller. "I will return then after school to talk with you about Elenore." He patted his daughter's head. "Auf Wiedersehen, Lorchen. You will wait here for me."

"Auf Wiedersehen, Papa," she answered, feeling suddenly very much alone.

"Welcome to Sumas School," said Miss Kent in a kindly voice. "We must find you a seat. By the way, what is that you have in the pail?" she continued, looking at the small blue pail that Lori was carrying in her hand. The words "Swift's Lard" were written in gold letters across the side.

"It's my lunch."

Miss Kent pointed to a shelf, "Well, you can put your lunch over there, Elenore." As Lori placed the pail on the shelf loaded with the brown bags and lunch boxes she heard several of the children snickering to themselves.

"Miss Kent, everyone calls me Lori. That's short for Elenore," she murmured, feeling timid and unsure of herself. Her stomach seemed to be one big knot as she observed all the children staring at her.

"Of course. Lori it is," replied Miss Kent, smiling. "We are in the middle of a grammar lesson on subjects and predicates. If you have any questions I will explain later."

As the teacher continued with her lesson Lori looked around the room. The furniture consisted of the students' and teacher's desks, a bookcase under the row of windows, a shelf for lunches and a long table at the back of the room. There was also a heater and a wood box containing large pieces of wood.

The girls in the class were wearing knee-length skirts or dresses of bright colors. She thought of her plain brown dress that reached to her ankles and sighed. The girls in the Mennonite school she had attended wore long dresses like hers, but here she felt like someone from another world.

She noticed, too, that all the girls wore their hair in varying lengths, some short, some shoulder length, but no one had long braids like hers. And although Mama had taken special care to braid it neatly this morning she would have settled for her ordinary mousy brown hair if only it could have been short.

Many of the girls were wearing knee high socks, not dark stockings like hers. And their shoes! She sighed again as she remembered shopping for shoes and seeing some beautiful brown and white saddle shoes in the store. How she had wanted a pair! But Mama said they were too impractical, and having been taught never to argue with her parents, she had settled for the plain brown ones.

The grammar lesson continued, and since Lori already knew the subject very well she felt free to continue her inspection. The children were of different sizes and Lori thought they must range in age from ten to fourteen. Half the students were boys, dressed in jeans or corduroy pants.

Her brown eyes came to rest on the girl directly across from her. Lori guessed that she was about twelve years old, the same age as she was. She had shoulder length curly blond hair that shone in the sun. Lori was sure it was the most beautiful hair she had ever seen. Her complexion reminded her of flowers in spring, and her cheeks matched the rose sweater she wore. Her blue eyes were the same color as her skirt and matching knee socks, and on her feet were beautiful saddle shoes. She even wore a gold wrist watch.

How pretty she is, Lori thought to herself, just as Miss Kent directed a question at the girl. "Please, Susie, what is the subject of sentence number four?"

Susie replied in a rather bored voice, "The man went."

"You should be aware by now, Susie, that subjects never contain action words or verbs, and *went* is a verb. Perhaps if you paid closer attention you would do better," said Miss Kent rather sternly.

"Would you like to try one, Lori? How about sentence number five," suggested the teacher.

"The red balloon," answered Lori. "*The balloon* is the subject and *is flying* is the verb."

"An excellent answer," praised Miss Kent. "I see you learned your grammar well at your other school."

Lori was elated by Miss Kent's kind words until she saw the scornful look on Susie's face. Her stomach felt strange again, so she sat with downcast eyes.

When the bell rang for morning recess everyone rushed outside. Not knowing what was expected of her, Lori lingered. "Put on your coat and join the other children on the playground," encouraged Miss Kent.

"Recess is a good time to get to know the other girls. Run along now."

On the playground some of the children were swinging. Others were playing ball or hopscotch. Lori leaned against the wall of the school and watched the others. Soon she saw a group of girls coming towards her. Susie, with her arm around another girl, was in the lead.

"Well, hello there, brainchild!" Susie's voice sounded rather mocking. "I'm Susie Chadsey. My father owns the store just down the road. Where do you live?"

"On the same road about a mile away." Lori had been glad someone came to talk to her, but Susie's remark started her stomach flipping again.

"Where do you come from anyway? Must be from somewhere across the ocean, because people here don't dress like you do. Your father has some queer accent. I could hardly understand him."

"We lived in the prairies. My parents did come across the ocean, but that was just before I was born. They speak German, but Papa is working very hard at learning English, although it is hard for grownups to unlearn their accent."

"I can't understand why our government is letting Germans into this country when we are at war with them! You do know Canada declared war on Germany a few months ago, don't you?" Susie turned to the other girls with her. "Can you imagine letting enemies into our country at a time like this?"

"We sure can't, Susie. It doesn't make sense. But Lori's family has been in Canada a long time, hasn't it?" answered Mary, a little timidly.

"That's right. We came long before the war started, and we are not from Germany, we only speak German, "replied Lori in an effort to defend herself and her parents."We love Canada and are very thankful to the government for giving us a new home. We are loyal Canadians."

"Well, you sure don't look like the rest of us, a Canadian with your long dress and long braids," said another girl.

Before Susie could continue, a blond boy whom Lori had noticed sitting in the eighth grade section of the classroom walked up to them. "Susie, how would you feel on your first day at a new school if someone said unkind things to you? Why don't you keep your feelings to yourself."

The bell rang, and as the children ran towards the classroom, Susie called after the boy, "What I say and do is none of your business, Harry Toop, so just leave me alone!"

Harry ignored her, and continued up the stairs with the other children.

At noon they all ate lunch at their desks. Lori opened her pail and took out her sandwich.

"What a funny way to bring your lunch, in a pail! And look at those thick slices of bread! That sure didn't come from our store," Susie said, staring at Lori's lunch.

"Mama baked it and it's hard to slice thin." Lori almost choked on her peanut butter sandwich as she spoke.

"Is that all you have to eat? No cookies or an apple?" asked Louise, one of Susie's friends sitting in front of her.

Lori nodded her head, and thought about what Mama said this morning, that until Papa finds work we are very thankful to have bread and peanut butter. There was a time when even peanut butter was a luxury.

At this moment Miss Kent looked up from the papers she was correcting. "That looks very good to me, Lori. I love homemade bread although I do not bake it myself. Could I have a little taste of it?"

Lori saw the children, some of whom had been snickering at Susie's remarks, stop and watch Miss Kent taste the bread.

"This is excellent," she remarked. "Be sure to tell your mother she makes very fine bread."

Lori smiled at Miss Kent, feeling the knot in her stomach easing just a little. She is wonderful. I love her already, Lori thought to herself.

Lunch over, everyone prepared to go outside. Susie commented to Lori in passing, "Can you to play hopscotch with such a long dress on? Isn't it kind of hard to hop on one foot? You can trip if your foot gets caught in your hem." She bounded out of the room, followed by Mary, Louise, and her group of girls.

Lori tagged after the other children, knowing the teacher wanted her to be on the playground. Since everyone was busy at something she sat down and leaned against the side of the building. She had neither the courage nor the desire to ask any group if she could join them.

She thought with longing of the friends she had left behind. How she wished Papa had never decided to move to British Columbia, away from the small community that had been the only home she knew. It was a safe place where everyone looked and talked as they did. How was she going to make friends with these girls all dressed in short skirts and saddle shoes? As long as Susie was so critical of her the other girls would do the same.

Then she remembered the struggle her parents had had merely to put food on the table for the three of them. Papa had tried unsuccessfully to find work. Since only seasonal work on the farms was available for him, Mama had to clean houses for other people to provide the bare necessities.

Neither of them was used to that kind of life. Mama had been a teacher in the old country and Papa a landowner with servants. How hard it must be for them! No wonder Papa wanted a place of his own once more.

Somehow she would have to make the best of it. She could not add to her parent's troubles by being unhappy. How could spoiled girls like Susie, who had everything, possibly understand?

With a new determination she got up when the bell rang and walked back into the classroom.

Two

When the daily arithmetic lesson was over Miss Kent set a vase containing some small sprigs on her desk. "I want you to sketch these pussy willows just as you see them. Use your pencil to give them texture and highlights," she said to the class.

Lori had never seen pussy willows before, and longed to touch them. They looked so soft and delicate, like the fur on the little gray kitten she had to leave behind in Manitoba.

Miss Kent must be able to read my mind, thought Lori, when her teacher broke off a small spray and handed it to her. "Coming from the prairies you have probably never seen pussy willows," she said in a kind voice. "Perhaps feeling them and seeing them at close range will help you to draw them."

"Oh, I thank you!" answered Lori, as she took the pussy willows and stroked them. They did feel exactly like the fur on her kitten, and a familiar warmth crept through her whole body. How could anything that was so soft and intricate grow when the air was still cold, she wondered. She was sure there must be some along the brook that meandered through their property, and she couldn't wait to find them.

Lori began reproducing this wonder of nature on her art paper. She was so engrossed she found it hard to realize the bell Miss Kent was ringing signaled the end of school for the day.

"Put your name on your work and place it on the table in the back of the room. If you have not completed your drawing there will be time tomorrow. Then get your belongings and line up to go home," Miss Kent said.

Alice, a rather stout girl, admired Lori's work as she was placing it on the table. "Your pussy willows look almost real. I wish I could draw like that!" she exclaimed.

"Why, thank you," Lori answered, her face lighting up with a smile. "They are so dainty and beautiful it was fun to draw them."

Susie, coming up behind them, remarked rather loudly, "So you're good at art, too, Lori. That ought to make you teacher's pet for sure."

"Let me see what you've done," said Alice quickly. "Yours is good too, Susie."

"It would be if I took more time," Susie answered. "But I have better things to do with my time than draw silly old pussy willows."

Harry, who was putting his drawing on the table, stopped to look at Lori's work. "Nice picture, Lori," he said as he cast a sideways glance at Susie. "They look almost real."

"Thank you, Harry," Lori said shyly She felt so much better until she heard Susie snicker.

"It seems you have added Harry to your fan club as well as Miss Kent."

Why was it, Lori wondered, that every time Susie spoke her stomach felt like one big knot? Her thoughts were interrupted by the opening of the door, and there stood Papa. His graying hair was neatly combed; his blue eyes looked searchingly about the room until he spotted her, when a smile lit up his face. He had on a clean pair of overalls, neatly mended at the knees, and even his boots, usually muddy from working the land, had been cleaned.

He stood at the door as the children filed by him, looking very unsure of himself. Miss Kent motioned them to the front of the room where she offered them each a chair.

"Thank you for coming, Mr. Mueller," she began." I can assure you right now that your daughter will have no academic problems. She seems to be bright and has an excellent grounding in all subjects we have covered today."

Lori's heart skipped a beat. It was good to hear those words from the teacher she already adored. Miss Kent smiled at her warmly. Her soft eyes seemed very brown in contrast to the white hair framing her face.

"I'm sure," continued Miss Kent, "that Lori feels somewhat overwhelmed by her new circumstances. It would help me to understand her better if you would tell me a little of your way of life and the school she attended before."

"Lori went to school near Winnipeg, where we lived in a Mennonite community. It was a Canadian school where they teach only English, but all the children were Mennonites, like Lori," said Papa.

"I really know very little about Mennonites and am eager to learn something of their background," Miss Kent said, encouraging him to continue.

"The Mennonites came first from Germany, but were asked by Katherine the Great of Russia to teach the Russian peasants how to farm. They went because the Tsarina promised them the chance to keep their religion, and she promised too that they should not have to fight in wars. They kept their German language, had their own schools, and some, like my family, became very rich. I would have to be honest and say we did not help the Russian peasants too much. When the Communist Revolution came we had to flee for our lives. The Canadian government took us in, and gave us a chance to pay back the cost of our trip later."

"I would be interested to know why you left your community in the prairies to come here to British Columbia," continued Miss Kent.

"I had owned much land in the Ukraine, and missed having land of my own," answered Papa. "Times were very hard in the prairies, and my wife, who had been a teacher, had to clean houses for other people so we could eat. I found very little work, just when the farmers needed help on the farms. I will say I studied the English language very hard while looking for work, even though I have a German accent and sometimes cannot think of the right words. When I heard about the Canadian government's plan to sell land with no money down it seemed like a gift from heaven. I'm sure others of my religion will follow."

"Well, I certainly wish you luck in your new land," was Miss Kent's sincere comment. "I do think the children will need a little time to become accustomed to Lori, her different dress and hair, and her reticence. The fact that your native tongue is German during a time we are at war with Germany may well make a difference. It is unfortunate that this is true, but children are influenced by their parents' attitudes, and right now our attitude towards Germans is influenced by the war. I am equally sure that as this community comes to know you these attitudes will change. You need to have a little patience." She smiled at Lori, as if to reassure her.

Lori noticed a very thoughtful look on her Papa's face. "I am happy to wait and let the community know us," he finally said. "We are honest, hard working people. But our religion tells us that it is not what we look like on the outside that matters, but how much trust we have in our God, and what we are like on the inside. We believe that to dress in plain clothes helps us to remember to put God first. Lori will not change in her dress. I want her to grow up in our Mennonite beliefs. Therefore I do not want her to take part in any parades or activities making war a glory. We believe that nobody has the right to kill for any reason. I thank you for seeing me." He got up, indicating that for him the discussion was now over.

During the whole conversation Lori never spoke. She had been taught never to contradict her elders, and with a sinking feeling she realized that her otherwise gentle and kind Papa would not relent where dress and hair style were concerned. His beliefs remained steadfast and unbending.

"Thank you for coming, Mr. Mueller," said Miss Kent, also rising. "It is obvious to me that you are very interested in Lori's welfare. I will certainly do what I can to help her make a satisfactory adjustment." She saw them to the door and Lori knew that she had found her very first friend in this strange new world.

On the way home Papa took his daughter's hand and held it in his own.

"Now tell me, my Lorchen, how was your first day? I am so pleased that you are such a good student, but of course I already knew that." There was unmistakable pride in Papa's voice. "Did you get to know any of the other children?"

"Well, Papa, I met Susie and Harry. Susie is the daughter of the store owner right there." She pointed to the building they were just passing where a blond girl was sitting on the porch. She appeared to be looking through a book and did not acknowledge them. Lori clutched her Papa's hand more tightly and continued, "She made some unkind remarks about the way I was dressed, about your accent, and wondered how the Canadian government could let us in here. Harry tried to set her straight, but he did not succeed."

"You must not let that upset you." Papa's voice was very gentle. "After all, God, who is very wise, led us to this land, and He will care for us. We must be loyal to our new country but hold with our beliefs, and show Him by the way we live how thankful we are. The children will learn to respect you, I am sure."

But I want more than respect, thought Lori to herself. I want to be part of their crowd, join in their games, be told their secrets, and just belong. Thoughtfully she looked about her. As if by magic her troubles vanished as she saw all about her the beauty of her new world.

"Look at those mountains all around us!" she cried excitedly. "Their snow covered peaks seem like guards for this whole valley. I cannot imagine how we lived without them all these years. Can you imagine, Papa, how beautiful it will be when everything bursts into bloom? I can't wait for spring! Do you know what kind of trees those are, Papa?" asked Lori. "They are so tall, and they seem to grow in clumps here and there."

"Those are cottonwoods. I am told they grow everywhere in this part of the country. The smaller ones you see along the brook, with white trunks are birch trees. We have many of both on our land." Papa's voice was filled with contentment.

"We are almost home where there is a surprise waiting for you," continued Papa rather smugly.

"Oh Papa, please tell me what it is!"

"If I told it wouldn't be a surprise, would it? You will just have to wait and see."

As they passed the last farm, their neighbor Mr. Manual, who was herding his cows into the barn, came over to the road to speak to them.

"Good afternoon, Mr. Manual. This is my daughter, Elenore, who arrived with her mother a few days ago. Today was her first day of school." Papa said, as Lori shook Mr. Manual's hand.

"I am so glad to meet you, Mr. Manual," said Lori as she smiled at the pleasant looking elderly man with sparkling blue eyes and graying hair.

"You speak very good English. You don't have an accent like your father. His English is quite good but I have trouble understanding him sometimes. Perhaps you can help him adopt our ways as well as our language.

"Lori has no accent because she was born in this country and learned English at school," Papa said seriously. "It is not hard for the young." Then, his tone changing to one of amusement, he continued. "We are trying. But it is hard for an older person to change accents. You will have even more trouble understanding my wife, because she speaks English poorly. It would be hard for me to speak English to her now when I fell in love with her and married her speaking German. I'm afraid we wouldn't understand each other very well."

"Why, I never thought of that," was Mr. Manual's thoughtful reply. "I'd hate to have to speak in a different language to my Maud. We have enough trouble as it is. Say, what's your first name anyway? Since we are neighbors we should be on a first name basis."

"Jacob is my name, after the great man who lived in Israel long ago."

"Well, Jake," Mr. Manual grinned. "I hope you don't mind if I call you Jake. Jacob sounds much too formal and Jake is easier for me to deal with."

Lori saw Mama walking across the street to join them. After Papa introduced her to Mr. Manual, Mama smiled and said, "I hear you talk so I come say hallo. You come see how house looks now? Have bread and jam?"

"I know you have been working so hard on it. I would love to see it, but I have little time now. I have been repairing my harrow this morning, but now I have to work on the fences. Another time, perhaps," answered Mr. Manual.

"I know not what harrow is," was Mama's puzzled reply.

"A harrow has teeth and is used to till the land after plowing. You may want to borrow it later this spring after the land is dry enough to plow."

Mama looked more puzzled than ever. "But my Jacob have teeth. He got teeth last year. They fit bad but we go back. The doctor fix."

The whole conversation sent Lori into gales of laughter. The idea of Papa borrowing Mr. Manual's teeth was incredibly funny. Mr. Manual was polite and tried not to laugh, while Papa patted Mama's head and explained that teeth were part of the harrow. Mama then joined in Lori's laughter. Mama finally said,"You keep your teeth. We use your harrow."

"Well, this proves you must teach your Mama to speak better English. By the way, young lady, I want you to know that you are welcome at our house any time. Maud and I have no children of our own, and it would be nice to have you visit once in a while. Our niece Jo comes every year for her Easter holidays, but that is only for ten days. Don't forget now." Mr. Manual started back to the barn.

"I thank you so much," Lori called after him. "I would love that." She now had two friends in this new world, and a pleasant warmth crept from her toes to the top of her head.

"And now to our surprise," said Papa as they turned into the path to their own home. "Just take a peek behind the house and you'll see them."

Three

Lori ran down the narrow path hewn out of the underbrush, around the shingled house that looked more like a shack than a home, stopped, and uttered an expression of pure joy. "Oh, Papa, they are adorable!" she cried. "They must be goats. I've seen them in picture books but never in real life." She stepped closer. "This one is trying to eat my coat, and that one seems afraid and wants to hide. My goodness, they must feel strange here! Can you let them loose? I know they hate to be tied up like that. Wherever did you get them? "

Papa looked very pleased. "No, we can't let them loose. They would run away. A farmer down the street gave them to me. He said they were too hard to milk. After supper we'll see if he's right. It will be wonderful to have real, fresh milk."

Lori petted the black goat, which nuzzled her arm rather timidly. Soon both goats walked over to a box in which Papa had put some of last year's grass, so dry it looked like hay.

"I'll have to build a fence for them, and a shed to keep them warm in the winter. But let's go in now. We'll milk the goats right after supper."

Lori was reluctant to leave the goats, but once they were out of sight she bounded happily into the house. "Oh Mama," she said, throwing her arms around her mother. "Won't it be great to have real milk? Maybe I can take them for a walk every day until Papa finishes the fence."

"Ach, ach, my Lorchen, please get slower. Ja, good goats. They so strong. You not walk, they pull. Now tell me, school." Mama was following Lori's lead and trying hard to speak English.

Lori noticed Mama's beautiful auburn hair tied in its usual neat roll in the back, but those stubborn little curls, as always, crept out from the coiffure and surrounded her whole face. I'm glad her hair won't stay tidy, thought Lori. It makes her look young and kind of impish.

School was the farthest thing from Lori's mind at the moment, so much had happened! "It was all right, I guess." Seeing Mama's concerned expression, she added quickly, "I have the most wonderful teacher, and it's easy, much easier than my other school was."

"Good, good, my little Lorchen. I want that you should be very happy here." Her brown eyes were sparkling as she continued, "New neighbor, Mrs. Manual, she bring something. She say cassole. She say I put in oven and keep warm." She walked over to the wood stove in the middle of the kitchen, opened the door, and pointed to a dish inside. The stove had obviously been scoured, but it still showed signs of wear in places. "It different, this cassole. I not know what inside it."

"Mama, that is a *casserole*. We learned in school that a casserole has a mixture of many things in it, all baked together. Maybe it is like our borscht where we mix everything together and cook it in water to make soup," Lori said, smiling at Mama's English. "Mama, it is good for us to speak English to one another. It helps you to learn the language.'"

"I try English," Mama said, and then added, "but sometimes I need speak own German. And to Papa only German when we alone or we have to split."

"I think you mean split up," Lori said, laughing. "I wouldn't want that, so just practice when we are all here. I know it will help."

Papa, who had been listening to them, looked at his wife and said, "I think it is a good plan to practice your English, Erna, but please do not start cooking the English dishes. I like our food just like we have always had it."

Mama placed the casserole in the middle of the table. "Hmm, soup plates or flat plates?" she asked as she walked over to the nearby open shelves, covered with shiny bright yellow oilcloth. Selecting three soup bowls, she placed them on the wooden table Papa had made. It too was covered with bright yellow oilcloth.

"Now we are ready," she continued, sitting down next to Papa on one of the two homemade benches." But first we thank God for this cassole, even if it is English."

"Father, we thank Thee for this meal, with which Thou hast blessed us this day," prayed Papa. "Mayst Thou bless it to our bodies."

Mama dished up the casserole with a large wooden spoon. Lori could see potatoes, carrots, peas, beans and cubes of meat in it.

Papa took one bite and began coughing. "Whatever it is in this casserole makes my throat burn," he complained. "Why do they have to mix everything up? I like my meat, potatoes and vegetables all apart, so I can tell what I am eating. And why put so much pepper in it? All I can taste is pepper."

"Please be not unhappy," answered Mama, laughing. "If no cassole, we have bread and boiled beans. We have not yet money for meat. So eat and like it."

Papa said not another word, and ate in resigned silence. Lori looked lovingly at Mama, for she knew that her way of making the best of all situations was just what Papa needed.

"Time to wash the dishes," said Mama. She went outside to the hand operated pump and brought in some water in a big pan, placed it on the stove to heat and turned to her daughter. "Lorchen, go help Papa milk goats. I wash dishes for you tonight."

Lori did not have to be asked twice. Selecting an empty pail, she bounded out of the door. Papa followed with a low stool. He stood for a moment not knowing where to begin, then resolutely placed the stool next to the goat. The goat kicked its legs and bounded forward. Every time Papa moved, the goat moved, too, until Lori remarked that in a book she had read goats were fed salt for a treat. She ran into the house and returned with a handful of salt.

"Now hold still, little Mandy, while Papa milks you. I will call you Mandy because that is one of my favorite names." she said to the brown and white goat. Gently she petted the goat, offering her salt. Mandy, subdued now, began licking the salt in Lori's hand. The goat's tongue tickled her hand so she could hardly bear it, but seeing Papa actually getting some milk into the pail, she held very still.

When the salt was gone Mandy gave one energetic kick, and the milk in the pail spilled all over. Papa muttered something in Russian, and Lori knew these were words he did not want her to understand. He always spoke Russian when he was upset, or when he wanted to tell Mama something Lori was not to share.

"Too bad, Papa! Just when you had quite a bit of milk in that pail. But don't worry; we'll try the other goat. She is much gentler." Lori turned to the black and white goat. "I named your friend Mandy so you will be Molly. Do you like your new name?" She petted Molly, and Papa could actually milk her on his first try.

When he was almost finished Mandy bounded over to Molly, butted Papa with her head so that he, the stool, and the pail all went flying. Just when Papa opened his mouth to say something in Russian again, Lori heard laughter, joyous, catching laughter.

There stood Mama at the side of the house, her long dress dragging along the ground because she was bending over, holding her head in her hands, and laughing. "Farmer give bad goats us," she said when she finally managed to talk. "I think you take them now back. Tomorrow oatmeal and no milk."

"I will teach those goats to stand still! I will make cuffs for their legs so they cannot kick," Papa said, smiling in spite of himself.

Lori, in the meantime, was tasting the tiny bit of milk left in the pail. She turned to Mama. "Ugh! You should try this! I don't see how anyone could drink it; It tastes strange and is very rich, like cream. I'd have to be dying of thirst before I'd swallow another mouthful of that!"

"People say we can get used to goat's milk and even learn to like it. Right now we do not have a problem. We have two milked goats and no milk." said Papa dryly. "But it is getting dark, and time to have our hour with God."

Mama got down a kerosene lamp from the shelf and lit it. Papa went into the adjoining bedroom, separated from the kitchen by a curtain strung across on a length of rope, and returned with the Bible. They sat down at the table and Papa read a chapter from Matthew. Then all three folded their hands as Papa led them in prayer.

"We thank Thee, God, for bringing us safely to this, our new home," Papa prayed. "Please guide us through the next few weeks. We thank Thee for helping me find work so that I can feed my family. And please help my daughter Lori to find happiness and friends at school."

So Papa is aware of the problems I am facing at school, thought Lori. He knows me well enough to know how troubled I am. A feeling of intense love for her father surged through her, and she silently thanked God for her parents.

"Bless our new home so that it is a place of peace, a place where we live in happiness together," continued Papa. "And we thank Thee, God, for the goats. Amen."

The end of the prayer brought the solemnity of the occasion to an abrupt halt, as all three joined in hearty laughter.

"Tonight go to bed early," Mama announced. "Papa clear brush tomorrow on a farm close by. I wash clothes." She pointed to the tin washtub and scrub board in one corner of the kitchen. "I make new dress for you, Lori. Good we bring old sewing machine."

"Could you make my new dress just a little shorter than the brown one I wore today, Mama? The girls at school wear theirs much shorter."

Before Mama could answer Papa said, "We do not hold with fashion. I do not want to see my Lorchen with her knees showing. It is just not seemly."

Lori's heart sank. Somehow she was sure God wouldn't mind if her knees showed just a little. But she said nothing.

"By the way, Mama, do you have an empty sack? I would like to take my lunch in a sack tomorrow. Then I can throw it away after I eat my sandwich."

Mama's expression was very puzzled as she went to a box under the shelves and pulled out a large burlap sack. "My Lorchen, why you want carry lunch in this?"

"Oh, Mama, you are funny! I mean a paper sack, a small one like you would get in a grocery store if you bought something small."

"No, I not have paper sack. The English is big muddle. I mix words up." Mama sounded genuinely discouraged. "I try to learn, but is very hard."

"You are doing just fine," said Lori, consoling her. "And now that you have no Germans to talk to except Papa and me you will learn very quickly. Speaking English to me will really help. Just wait and see."

That night in bed Lori thought about the events of the day. Her bed was separated from her parents' bedroom by a blanket nailed to the ceiling, to give both her and them some privacy.

Her homemade mattress of burlap filled with straw felt comfortable with the flannel sheet over it. Her whole body relaxed under the soft featherbed. How glad she was that this goose feather cover was one of the things they had been able to bring with them. It felt cozy to pull her knees under her flannel nightgown and snuggle under the warm coverlet.

She thought about spring just around the corner. How beautiful the whole countryside would be when all the trees and bushes came to life. She thought about the brook just behind their house with the spring that bubbled ice cold water from somewhere in the ground. She was sure there would be frogs and tadpoles in the brook. Soon the birds would be returning, especially the swallows would come back. Papa said many swallows came from the south in the summer months. He had seen their empty nests on the eaves of Mr. Manual's barn. And majestic mountains would be guarding it all.

Then she thought about school, and the day just ahead. That same old queasy feeling returned once more. Would school always be another day to get through? Or would she actually come to look forward to it?

She folded her hands in prayer. Oh, God, please be with me tomorrow, and help me get along in my new school. And if Thou doesn't mind my knees showing just a little, please let Mama make my new dress just a wee bit shorter.

Then she snuggled under the coverlet, and next thing she knew Mama was calling her for breakfast.

Four

The air smells like spring, said Lori to herself on her way to school, but I feel like turning around and going back home. I'd rather follow this brook and see where it leads. But Papa would say that is a coward's way out.

She was kicking rocks as she walked along the graveled road, not even caring if she scuffed her new brown shoes. It had been eight-thirty when she left home, and if she walked slowly enough she would get there just when the bell rang. That would suit her very well.

Three boys passed her, and though she had seen them at school, they hurried by and did not acknowledge her presence.

The two room schoolhouse loomed before her, its gray exterior giving it a cold and foreboding look.

Children were lined up to enter, the younger ones in one line, and the older ones in another. No one spoke to her as she followed the older children into the classroom. Except for a warm greeting from Miss Kent and a shy smile from Alice, she was totally ignored.

During the Social Studies lesson the topic of war arose. The students discussed the reason Canada was fighting Germany. All sixth, seventh and eighth graders participated in the discussion.

"Germany has no right to occupy the countries she has taken over. Austria, Poland, and Czechoslovakia have a right to be free," said Harry. "It is only right that we should join Great Britain in helping them."

"Hitler wants to conquer the world, my father says," said Mary. "If we don't stop him now we'll all be conquered."

"How do you feel about this war, Lori?" Miss Kent asked. "I feel even though your parents are of German origin they love their adopted country and would do anything to help."

"They would support Canada, but they would not fight. Our religion teaches us that it is wrong to kill another human being for any reason. But they would help in any other way they could."

Several of the children gasped at Lori's words. Before Miss Kent could reply Lori continued, "I would become a nurse and take care of those wounded in this terrible war," she said as she looked around at all the shocked faces. "I would even go to the front, if necessary, to take care of the injured there."

"There are many ways of serving our country," continued Miss Kent. "And that would be an admirable way of doing it. I see that it is time for recess, so get ready for the playground."

At recess Lori was surrounded by children of both sexes. "You mean your parents actually believe that it is wrong to fight for your freedom?" Susie asked in an astonished voice. "So they'd let everyone else fight for them while they were home and safe? Isn't that kind of cowardly?"

"They are not cowards. In the First World War my Papa served with the Medical Corps and was near the front all the time. We believe that if everyone felt as we did there would be no war."

"And let the Hitlers of this world run all over us?" said Mary.

"We did try negotiating and none of it worked, so what else is there to do?" said one of the sixth grade boys.

"I think we should all respect Lori's beliefs. In this free country everyone has a right to their convictions.

After all, isn't that what we are fighting for?" added Harry, a serious expression in his blue eyes.

"Well, you go ahead and respect them. I can't," Susie said, and turning on her heel she walked away, her head in the air, followed by her group of friends.

Harry walked over to Lori when the other children had left. "I liked what you said, so don't let Susie upset you. She needs a lesson in thinking of someone besides herself." He smiled warmly at Lori as he walked away.

Alice, who had also stayed, walked over to Lori. "I'm sorry," she said sincerely. "I wish there was something I could say or do to help. The kids don't like me either, because I am fat and my father is called the town drunk, so I do know how you feel. "

Lori looked intently at Alice, feeling a surge of compassion for her. "I'm sorry, too," she said simply. "But Papa would tell us to have patience, and that God knows what's best for us. Only sometimes this is not very evident."

The two girls walked over to the swings and sat there slowly swinging until recess was over. Though neither of them talked, Lori felt a closeness to Alice. Their problems were very different but the outcome was the same. The other children wanted nothing to do with them.

Before lunch Miss Kent asked the children to finish an assignment on the geography of British Columbia that was due the next day.

"Do you have any books at home to help you?" she asked Lori. Since Lori had none Miss Kent allowed her to work on the assignment during the lunch break. Lori considered it an act of kindness, and was relieved not to have to go outdoors and face the other children.

After school, Susie, who had said nothing further to Lori all day, caught up with her. "Since we are practically neighbors why don't I come home with you and meet your parents," she said, a big smile on her face. "I'll just run in and tell Mom where I'm going." Lori merely nodded, but thought it odd that Susie wanted to visit her home, especially after her outburst this morning.

All the way home Susie talked about the high school they would be attending in two years. "I can't wait," she said. "It will be so different from this one horse school where all the kids live on farms, except for me. I'll meet other kids whose dads own stores and have businesses. It will be very important to dress just right, especially if you want to attract the attention of boys, I mean to find friends, and especially a boyfriend. I imagine I'll have a whole new set of kids to chum around with."

"Don't you like the friends you have now?" asked Lori, dumbfounded. "You seem to be very popular."

"Oh, they'll do for now, but they aren't really in my class. I want to go to parties with the kids in Chilliwack, where the junior high is. We'll have to go by bus every day, you know. We'll have to dress right to fit in there."

Lori thought about her own clothing and the poverty they were living in right now. What chance did she have if clothes were all that mattered? Surely there were children somewhere who would like her just as she was.

"Well, I hope junior high is all you are hoping for," is all she could think of to say. She found it very hard to talk to Susie. She had never even thought about the things Susie was discussing. Except for the groups at church, she had never attended a party or thought of boys. Although she had to admit to herself that Harry, who had come to her defense a couple times, was both understanding and good looking. If she ever had a boyfriend it would have to be someone like him. Too bad he would be going to high school in the fall.

"Don't you like Harry?" Lori asked Susie. "I think he'd be a good boyfriend for any girl. He is smart and good looking too."

Susie stared at Lori. "So you have a crush on Harry, do you? He's good looking but he's only interested in learning. He doesn't even look at girls and he always does the right things."

It was Lori's turn to stare. "What's wrong with doing the right things?"

"Nobody likes goody-goodies. They like kids who like to have fun and don't care so much about grades, and do a few things behind their parents' backs now and then. That's the only way to have fun," explained Susie.

Lori said nothing more. Where she came from all the children followed the school rules, and the ones who didn't were looked down upon. What a strange place this British Columbia was. Or was every place like that except when you lived among Mennonites?

Susie chatted on about her hopes for high school, but Lori hardly listened. Too much was racing through her mind. Finally, they reached the path Papa had hewn out of the underbrush surrounding her home.

"Here we are," Lori said as they turned into the path.

"This is the path to your house? You're kidding! How do you ever manage to keep your shoes clean? No wonder they're dark brown. I'll have to clean mine before school tomorrow, that's for sure. Couldn't your dad put some gravel or something on this?" She waved her hand at the path, where bits of root were protruding in quite a few places.

The knot in Lori's stomach suddenly disappeared, and for the first time anger welled up inside her. Did this critical girl have no understanding at all of other people's problems and circumstances?

"We have only been here a few days," was her curt retort, "and Papa did the best he could during the month he was here without us. This path suits us very well for now."

Susie did not appear to notice Lori's anger, for she uttered another gasp when she suddenly spied the shingled house in the clearing. "That is your house? Why, it's just a shack, not even painted. How can you possibly live in that?"

"We manage very well," Lori answered in a voice once more quiet, but very determined. "We were given it by someone who no longer needed it. Papa moved it here with the help of our neighbor Mr. Manual and his horse. It's only for the time being. After we have been here a while I'm sure we'll build a new one. We work very hard and we save all we can.

Lori heard Mama's voice as she opened the door. "I hear you bring a friend. Come, come in."

Lori, followed by Susie, saw Mama ironing on the kitchen table, and ran over to hug her. "Mama, I would like you to meet Susie, who lives down the street near the school."

"It nice to meet you," Mama said as she placed the iron back on the stove. She returned Lori's hug warmly, smiled her special smile, wiped her forehead where all the little curls had crept out again, and straightened the apron she wore over her long brown dress.

Lori noticed that Susie barely heard her. She wore an expression of horror as she stared at all parts of the room. She was looking at the walls, where two by fours were evident every few feet because the inside wall had not yet been built, at their utensils on the plain shelves with no doors , and at the wood stove with a big pan on it. Her eyes wandered next to the benches and stools Papa had made and came to rest on the curtain partitioning the bedroom.

"Oh, I'm glad to meet you," answered Susie at last. "My father owns the store down the street."

"Maybe you like goat milk and piece of bread with peanut butter?" offered Mama. "You be hungry after school."

"I see Papa finally managed to get some milk from the goats," said Lori. "I almost wish he hadn't. That milk is awful. Just give me the bread please, Mama. Want some, Susie?"

Susie, who was still staring around the room, merely nodded.

"This is really good bread, much better than the bread in our store." It was the first kind thing Lori had ever heard Susie say.

"Mrs. Mueller," she added. "Mother is looking for someone to help in the house while she works in the store. If you want I'll tell her you need the job. I think you need the money and you could bake us bread like this?"

"I want work very bad, "Mama answered."My husband find very little work so I help. I work hard. Do what your mother needs do."

"It's as good as settled." Susie sounded as though she were the one making the decision. "Lori, do you have a room where we could sit and visit?"

"It's only a cubbyhole in Mama' and Papa's bedroom, but we can sit on the bed."

Once again that look of horror crept over Susie's face as Lori pulled aside the blanket and motioned to Susie to sit on her bed.

Susie sat down, stared around her, and wondered, "How are you ever going to bring friends home if you do not even have one little place that is private? And where do you hang your clothes? I have a large closet at home just full of clothes."

"I fold my clothes neatly and put them on this shelf. You know, Susie, everyone isn't as fortunate as you are." Again there was anger in Lori's voice. "As I said before, we just need some time to improve our circumstances. Perhaps seeing how we must live right now will help you learn to count your own blessings." Suddenly Lori felt sorry for Susie. She wondered how Susie's family would cope if their own circumstances changed, for Susie's whole world revolved around the things she owned.

"Well, there is no place to visit and nothing to do so I'll be going home. My mother will need my help in the store." With a quick goodbye to Mama and a "See you tomorrow" directed at Lori, she walked quickly out the door.

"Ach, girl have bad manners. She snotty girl. She rude to not stay longer. Our house not fancy. It is clean." Mama sounded annoyed.

Lori laughed in spite of herself. "Mama, I think you mean snooty. I do think Susie feels superior to us, but for some reason many of the children at school do whatever she wants. I'm sure by tomorrow everyone at school will know all about us."

"Ach, Lorchen, you God's gift to Papa and me."

"Mama, I remember your telling me about my brother and sister who did not live even twenty-four hours. And once the Revolution started there was nothing to eat in the Ukraine because the communists took everything. You had to escape just to save your lives. When I was born just after you came to Canada, you promised God that you would bring me up to be honest and to trust Him. I also remember you telling me you kept asking the nurse if I was still alive. She couldn't understand why you were so worried since I was a fat nine pound baby!"

Mother smiled. "God give me smart baby girl. I am glad you are my daughter, and not that Susie!"

"Oh, Mama, I love you and I thank God you and Papa are my parents!   But do you think God really cares if my hair is long or short, and if my clothes are dark or cheery and bright?" Lori looked beseechingly at her mother.

"I do not know if God cares. Papa cares. You be fine and happy on inside, not care about outside. God says man head of family. Papa is good man."

"Do you think I don't know that, Mama? I love him so much!" said Lori fervently. "But can't he bend just a little sometimes? He is so stubborn!"

"Maybe good reasons," said Mama after some thought. "See Susie is pretty outside. Snotty inside."

Lori said no more. When Papa came home, dirty and tired, she ran happily to meet him.

Five

The month of March was almost over. Spring uncovered new surprises every day, and Lori never tired of all the discoveries she was making. The birches and cottonwoods were promising new foliage, crocuses were up around the school, and buds were unfolding everywhere. The frogs were croaking in the brook, and the grass was a carpet of luscious green.

As the weather warmed Lori began exploring the meadow beyond the brook. Wildflowers were starting to emerge everywhere, and the meadow grass was interspersed with many patches of clover. Later in the year she planned to bring a blanket, spread it out, and dream her dreams in these new and private surroundings. When she trudged through this fairy tale world problems disappeared, frustrations vanished, and she was filled with peace.

The goats had become accustomed to their new way of life, and grazed contentedly inside the fence Papa had built for them. Papa had managed to milk them, and Lori had become accustomed to their milk. Mama even made cheese from the milk, delicious cheese that tickled one's taste buds and was especially good on Mama's bread.

Mama worked at the Chadsey house every afternoon, and brought home many leftover treats. She found the Chadseys kind and congenial, but shook her head emphatically every time the subject of Susie arose. "That girl is terrible spoiled!" she would say. "Her mother and father not say no to her, she do what she want. She need servants all the time."

Papa was busy from morning until after the sun set. Not only did the farmers hire him to help with repairing barns and fences, but he had begun many projects on their own place. He was clearing a place for a garden, had already planted peas, a crop that could be planted early in the spring, and was as excited as a little boy when they began coming up.

He had also built Lori a shelf in her cubbyhole, one where she could keep her schoolbooks, her journal and the poetry she sometimes wrote. Papa had promised that this was her private shelf, off limits to both him and Mama. Writing in her journal was a great comfort to Lori, for here she could unreservedly express her frustrations and joys. It was like confiding in a good friend, one who always listened and understood.

Lori spent much time in Mr. Manual's barn, watching him milk his cows and do his chores. She loved his warm smile and down to earth way of talking, and she felt he paid her the greatest compliment when he asked her to call him Uncle Charlie. He, in turn, had nicknamed her "Brown Eyes" because, he said, she had the prettiest brown eyes he had ever seen.

Her parents had more money to spend. Their daily fare now included butter, meat, apples and even puffed wheat. The first time Lori had eaten it instead of oatmeal she wondered if that was how manna had tasted to the Israelites. It was so good she had three helpings! The resulting stomach ache had taught her that even good things have to be taken in moderation.

School was the only black spot in Lori's world, except for Harry. She smiled to herself as she remembered the times Harry had come to her defense when Susie was needling her. Sometimes, when she was walking home, Harry joined her. His farm was a few miles down the same road, and he would walk with her until she reached her gate. They usually discussed something they were studying at school, and since Lori was not used to conversing with boys, he did most of the talking. Lori was glad her Papa had not noticed because she knew he would not approve of her friendship with a boy.

Except for Alice, Lori had no girlfriends. Alice's drinking father and her excessive weight probably had something to do with her lack of friends, but Lori was thankful to have Alice to talk to and walk with at recess. Susie and her crowd ignored her, except to make unkind remarks like "How could you do such a good job on that assignment in that crowded shack with no place to work?" or "We're playing tag but your dress is too long, and Alice is too fat to run."

One day, when the teacher had read Lori's composition to the whole class, Susie cornered her at recess and said, "You ought to teach your mother how to speak English. I can't believe she was once a teacher. She seems to be unable to learn proper English."

"English is not the only language in the world, you know. I wonder how you would do in a foreign country yourself?" was Lori's comment. For once Susie had no answer.

The girls' conversation usually stopped when Lori and Alice were within earshot. They nudged each other and snickered, causing Lori's stomach to do flips. The two girls spent most of their recesses walking aimlessly around the grounds or sitting on the swings.

Alice was a good friend, but Lori felt more compassion for her than respect or admiration. Alice found learning very hard, and even with Lori's help, did not improve. She never had her homework done, and when Lori questioned her she said their house was too noisy because her dad was drunk all the time.

One day Mary, one of Susie's friends, was having a party. "Would you like to come?" she asked Lori. "My older brother is home on leave from the army and I would like to show him off."

"What!" exclaimed Susie, who was within earshot, "You're going to introduce your brother to someone who doesn't believe in war or fighting? That would be a great insult to him. After all, he is willing to lay down his life for his country, and he doesn't need cowards around."

"I don't think Lori is a coward. She just believes war is wrong. That's her religion." Mary looked very uncomfortable as she tried to defend Lori's position.

"Well, if she comes I'm not coming!" Susie almost screamed. "I have too much respect for Canada and what we're fighting for."

Harry, who had been listening to the conversation, turned to Susie and said, "You don't know the meaning of the word respect, Susie Chadsey. I wonder if you have ever thought about any person besides yourself.

You can respect others, even if you do not agree with them. Try just listening to different people's sincere beliefs. Perhaps you will learn something."

Susie gave Harry a scornful look and began walking away.

Lori turned to Mary. "Thank you so much for the invitation, Mary, but I will be busy tonight," she said simply, her heart going out to Mary for wanting to include her in the party. How were any of these girls going to be her friends as long as Susie was around to rule over them like a queen? Thank you, God, for Harry and his courage, Lori thought to herself. Too bad he would be going to high school in the fall.

One day after school Mama greeted Lori at the door with a large package. "This for you, Lorchen. This for you!" she called when Lori was only half way up the path.

"Oh, Mama, do you know where it came from? Why would I get such a big package in the mail? Is it really addressed to me?" Lori's voice was full of excitement.

Eagerly, she took the package, reading the return address. "Why, it's from Tante Hedwig in Toronto! Can you imagine what she would send me? I have never even met her."

"Don't stand and stare like a cow! Open it!" Mama was as excited as her daughter.

Lori slowly untied the string with great care, and then removed the wrapping paper with shaking hands. Next she opened the big cardboard box.

"They're skirts and sweaters, Mama, with knee socks to match! Can you believe this! Four skirts and four sweaters, all in gorgeous colors! And here's a note." Lori's joy knew no bounds.

"Dear Lori," she read to Mama. "The daughter of the doctor I work for is two years older than you are. She has outgrown these clothes. I thought you might be able to use them. Although I have never seen you, I am sure they will look very nice on you."

"Oh Mama, they look just like new! I'm going to try on this red plaid skirt, white sweater and white knee socks. Aren't you happy for me, Mama?" She raced into her cubbyhole, sweater in hand.

She returned just when Papa opened the door. "What is the meaning of all this?" Papa's puzzled look sent chills down Lori's spine. In her joy she had forgotten about Papa's strict dress code.

"Papa, they are skirts, sweaters and knee socks Tante Hedwig sent by mail. She felt certain I could use these. As you can see, the skirts are too long for the knee socks, but Mama and I can shorten them." Lori was afraid, even as she spoke, that this would never happen.

Papa's usually gentle face turned white, his eyes blazed angrily as they rested on the bright clothes on the kitchen table. "Since when do we dress ourselves so we look good on the outside? Look at you, my daughter! You are so beside yourself because of these clothes that you have forgotten all you have learned. You look ready to go to a dance, or down the street to find some boys. Do you not know that all these things make you forget your God? Why, you look just like Susie Chadsey! And in clothes like that you will soon be like her!" Papa sat down on the bench, a scowl on his face.

Mama straightened her apron as if to gather courage, turned to Papa and said gently, "Our Lori a good girl. She not is bad because she wear clothes like other girls. Maybe she be happier at school if not so different." Her eyes were pleading as she looked at Papa.

Papa returned the look with fire in his eyes. "So now you, who have always held with our ways, are willing to throw them out because we no longer live among our people? You think that our daughter will be happier if she looks the same as everyone else? We will say no more about it. The Bible says I am the head of this house. As that head I decide that Lori will not wear these clothes. I could not live with myself if I let her wear them."

Papa got up, visibly shaken, got a book from the bedroom, and began reading.

Mama started making preparations for dinner, her usual gaiety gone as she bustled about the kitchen without another word.

Lori, with one final longing glance at the clothes on the table, quietly retreated to her cubbyhole.

She wanted to cry, but no tears would come. She wanted to plead with Papa, but she had been taught never to oppose him. Suddenly she felt tired, too tired to find solace in her meadow.

Then she saw her friend, the journal, on the shelf. She picked it up, opened it, and began to write:

Dear Diary,

I am so very confused, my friend. I love Papa, but sometimes I want to scream at him in the loudest voice I can find. Today is one of those days. No matter how hard I try I cannot see why I can't wear those beautiful skirts and sweaters Tante Hedwig sent me. I think if I looked prettier on the outside I would feel prettier and be kinder and happier on the inside too.

It breaks my heart to own those gorgeous clothes and not be able to wear them. I admit I want to look like the other girls. I feel like defying my father and wearing them anyway.

But I know I will not do that, just like Mama kept quiet when she knew she had said enough. That's the worst of it; I'm causing my mother and my father to disagree.

So, dear diary, I will wear my same old long dresses, hating every minute of it, and be obedient to Papa.

But in my heart I feel that Papa is rigid and unreasonable. I do not think that God cares one bit what I wear, as long as I obey Him. And, my dear diary, I will never be like Susie! That I can promise you!

Your very sad Lori.

She heard Mama call her to set the table for supper. As she entered the kitchen she saw Mama neatly putting the new clothes back into the box and putting the box on the floor under the shelves.

Dinner was the quietest meal they had ever eaten.

Six

The days went by slowly, as spring uncovered new surprises every day and continued to clothe the countryside, until every bush and tree was a soft, yellowish green. The snow on the mountains was gradually decreasing, and the meadow was alive with dandelions, buttercups and clover.

None of this thrilled Lori as it had when she first came. She spent much time in the meadow just staring into space. She took a pad with her to write about the beauty all around her, but her heart was not in it, and when she returned home her pad was still empty.

There was a cloud over the household too. The easy and close relationship with Papa had suffered a subtle change. Lori was as respectful as ever to Papa, but her feeling for him had changed. She did not spontaneously tell him of the happenings in her life as she used to, and there was none of the usual display of affection between them.

Mama tried to talk to her, but Lori did not wish to discuss the clothes. Whenever Mama began Lori cut her off, unable somehow to tell her Mama that this time Papa had gone too far, and that the box sitting under the shelf was the reason for her reticence. Mama seemed to sense this and finally put the box away in her own bedroom.

At school things didn't fare much better. Lori did all her work and all her assignments, but made very little effort at them. She stayed most often to herself and was often very short with Alice, who could not understand what had happened to her friend.

One day Miss Kent asked Lori to stay in at recess to discuss an assignment. When the other children had gone she made a quick remark about one of the sentences in her assignment, then turned to Lori with a concerned look on her face and said, "I have noticed that you seem to be more withdrawn than you were when you first arrived. Your work is still good, but your compositions, for instance, lack the spontaneity they once had, and you make no effort make friends with the other children. Would you like to talk to me and tell me what is troubling you?"

Lori felt love for her teacher welling up inside her. So Miss Kent had noticed that she was troubled. How she would have liked to tell her about the box of clothes and of Papa's reaction to it. But she felt Miss Kent might find it necessary to speak to her parents in order to help her. This was far too risky, so she said simply, "I'm all right. Everything is just very strange still. I'll try to do better."

"If you ever want to talk, remember that I am always here and willing to listen."

"I will remember, and I thank you," Lori said simply. "May I go outside now?"

On the playground Lori went by a group of girls excitedly talking. "It sounds like a wonderful party, Susie," said one of them." Are you really going to have boys there?"

"I sure am," Susie answered, "and we're going to play all kinds of games like Spin the Bottle and Post Office. My parents promised they would stay out of our way. And I'll make sure that they do. Well, look who's coming! Too bad your parents are so straight-laced that you can't even have fun like the rest of us. Don't you ever get bored doing your schoolwork and talking to your goats? I'd still ask you but I don't want to get in trouble with your parents."

Lori merely smiled as she went by, but she knew that her smile was not sincere at all. She didn't really want to go to Susie's party, but she would have liked an invitation. How she longed for a friend who would truly understand her.

On the way home she heard footsteps behind her, and a voice that called, "Wait for me, Lori, so we can walk together as far as your place."

Lori tuned to see Harry behind her. His blond hair was rather tousled as though he had been hurrying; his blue eyes looked intently at her as he slowed down, still out of breath. He smiled at her then, and Lori's heart skipped a beat as it always did when Harry sought out her company. She knew that her papa wouldn't approve of any friendship she might have with a boy, but so far he hadn't seen them together. She was doing something behind Papa's back, but after the episode with the skirts and sweaters, she decided to keep Harry a secret.

"Hi! You sure are a hard one to catch up to! You really should enter the fifty yard dash on Sports Day. I've wanted to ask you if you would like to work on our science project with me. I think it would be fun to work on the vegetation of this region since there is so much of it, or have you already picked a topic?" Harry smiled warmly at her.

Lori was completely taken aback. "You mean you actually want to work with me, you want to do that project with me as your partner? Why, you are an eighth grader, almost in high school, and I'm only in grade six."

"Yes, I do. I've never done a project with anyone else before, because there has never been anyone who has the same interest in nature. But you really do. Your compositions that the teacher has read to us really show your love of nature. Well, what do you say?"

Lori felt that old knot in her stomach once more. Wouldn't all those kids begin to make fun of Harry if they saw them working together? Then he would surely regret it. She tried to put all this into words as kindly as she could. "Harry, you see how the kids treat me. They make fun of my clothes, my parents, and my beliefs. They would tease you too if you worked with me."

"Do you think I care? The kids think I'm strange as it is. They tease me because I care so much about my studies. But one day I will have a real profession while they will still be here on the farms. And you will have a profession too, Lori. You have the ability to go far." Lori saw real admiration in his eyes.

"How can I go far, or even go to college one day when my parents have to struggle just to make ends meet? Where would we ever get the money to send me to any school anywhere?" Lori looked at Harry with a defeated and hopeless expression on her face.

"I know you have had your problems with Susie and her crowd. I know they are having a big party tonight and that you weren't invited. For that matter, neither was I, and nothing could bother me less. Do you really want to go and listen to all that ridiculous chatter? You know, I don't think of you as a quitter, Lori Mueller, but right now you sound like one. You will grow up, be able to live your own life, and do your own thing without having to live up to what your parents think you should be. For goodness sakes, your parents are fine people who are hung up on their old country ways. Those ways will not always have to be yours. Once you are a little older you will be able to pick your own values. As far as college is concerned, you are smart enough to get all kinds of scholarships."

Lori stared at Harry. How well he understood the problems she was having. It all sounded so simple, listening to him. She smiled at him warmly and said with feeling in her voice, "Thank you for the pep talk, Harry. I really needed that. I will think hard about all the things you have said. And I'd love to do a project with you. I will work very hard. It will be great to study the vegetation of this beautiful country in depth. Well, here's my place. I'll see you tomorrow at school. Thanks again." Lori could think of nothing more to say. Was it because Harry was one of the few older boys that he understood her so well? He also had a quick mind and read a great deal. Perhaps that was another reason.

"Since our Easter holidays begin on Friday we'll start as soon as they are over. Be sure you keep your eyes open and find whatever information you can during our holidays. I'll do the same." Harry continued on his way as Lori turned into the path to her house.

In the house Lori said a warm hello to Mama and went directly to her room to think. Sitting on her bed, she realized that Harry had planted a hope, one that would help her through many dark moments. She respected and loved her parents so much, but she could not agree with some of the rigid beliefs Papa held about dress and behavior. There was a way out. She would not always be twelve years old, and the day would come when she could dress as she pleased. She would work hard as Harry had suggested, and perhaps it would be possible for her to go to college one day.

She heard Papa coming into the kitchen and went shyly to greet him. Some of her anger seemed to have left her, as she realized that in his own way he was doing what he thought was right for her. She realized, in that moment, how very deep her love for her parents was. This really was much more important than the way she was dressed.

"Did you have a good day at school, my Lorchen?" Papa asked. He hadn't called her my Lorchen in quite a while.

"Harry, one of the boys at school, asked me to work on a project with him. We are planning to study the vegetation of this region. He is in the eighth grade and the best student in the class so it should be a very good project."

"You know," Papa said, "that I do not want that you should have a boyfriend when you are still so young."

"He is not my boyfriend," Lori said quickly. "He just thinks I love the outdoors like he does and we could do a good science project on the vegetation here. And anyway, none of the girls have asked me."

"See to it that it is all science, as you call it, and that you are never alone with him," Papa said rather sternly.

Lori chose to ignore the last remark. Instead, she turned to her mama. "Mama, would you mind if I went over to talk to Uncle Charlie for a while?"

"You really like him, don't you?" Mama commented. "Tell him hallo from us."

Sitting on the milking stool, watching Mr. Manual milk his cows, Lori felt a sudden need to really talk to this friendly man. "Uncle Charlie, I need someone to talk to. I was going to talk to Miss Kent, my teacher, the other day but I was afraid she would say something to my parents. I know you would not if I asked you not to." Lori looked beseechingly at him.

"Of course I will listen. But would you please stop apologizing for wanting to do so. And since we are such good friends I can keep a secret when you ask me to." There was a merry twinkle in Mr. Manual's eyes.

"Oh, I'm glad. I am in enough trouble as it is. You see I got a box of pretty clothes from my aunt in Toronto a few weeks ago, but Papa wouldn't let me wear them because he thought they were not in keeping with our religion. I have been kind of angry at him ever since. I hate wearing these long dark dresses. But Papa never changes his mind where his beliefs are concerned so I guess I'm stuck with them."

"You are a pretty girl even in those long dresses. Not being a religious man myself, I do not understand your father's feeling about your clothes. But I do know your father is a good and honest man and is doing what he thinks is right for you. I have also found him to be very stubborn. If I get the chance and can work it into the conversation, I'll talk to him."

"It's not only that," Lori continued. "Harry Toop asked me to work on a science project with him on plants in this area. My papa doesn't approve of that either. He just told me I should never be alone with a boy, and we won't be able to find samples if we are never alone."

"Maybe I have a solution for that one," Uncle Charlie said. "You know, on Friday your Easter holidays will start. My niece Jo will be here to spend them with Maud and me. I have a feeling you and she will like one another. And with Jo there helping you find samples, you and Harry would not be alone. Besides, it will be a nice rest from school for you."

Lori gave her friend a hug, got up from the stool and helped him feed the young calf that had just been weaned from its mother.

In bed that night Lori thought about the party going on at Susie's house. It didn't seem to matter so much any more that she hadn't been invited. She thought about Harry and his pep talk. He really was the only boy in the whole school that she admired. Maybe they would become friends working on that project together. It was the first time any boy had paid attention to her, and it felt good. He really seemed to care about how she felt and to understand some of her confused emotions.

She remembered her talk with Uncle Charlie and wondered if he would be able to get through to Papa. Lori really doubted it, but it was so nice of him to try.

Just before she fell asleep Lori found herself thinking about Jo. If she was anything like her Aunt and Uncle she would be wonderful. And in just a few days Easter holidays would begin.

Seven

"Where is everyone? I've been banging and banging on your door forever and It's cold out here."

Lori heard what sounded like a young girl's voice as she finished dressing for breakfast. It was Good Friday, the first day of her Easter holidays, and since the Muellers considered this a very sacred day, neither Mama nor Papa was working. They had all slept in, and were just preparing for a breakfast of bacon and eggs, a very special treat.

Lori dressed quickly, her long hair still hanging unbraided about her shoulders, and hurried to the door. She opened it to be greeted by a girl about her own age dressed in a pair of blue jeans. "Well, it's about time! Some farmers you are! Uncle Charlie has been up since five o'clock, and it's already eight! I'm Jo, the niece he told you about. And you must be Lori, the wonder girl Uncle Charlie raves about."

The visitor's blue eyes were flashing mischievously, her shoulder length red hair flying in the morning breeze. Her whole demeanor was one of amusement as she impulsively threw her arms around Lori. "Don't mind me, but I feel as though I know you already, and am so glad Uncle Charlie finally has a neighbor my own age, especially one that I can explore the countryside with. You do like exploring, don't you? In the city where I live there's nothing to explore. Out here I feel as if I've just been let out of a cage."

"Hello, Jo. Yes, I'm Lori. Why don't you come in?" said Lori when she could finally get a word in. "We are about to have breakfast. Would you like to join us?"

Lori ushered the girl inside, noticing as she did so that Jo showed no surprise at the unfinished walls or the crude kitchen furniture. Mama was frying bacon and eggs on the stove, and Papa was sitting at the table, a Bible open before him.

"Mama and Papa, I would like you to meet Jo, Uncle Charlie's niece, who is here from Vancouver. May she have breakfast with us?"

"I very glad to meet you, Jo, "responded Mama."Yes, yes, breakfast. And it good you have red hair. Now I feel God not pick me alone. In Ukraine red hair thought bad sickness. Nobody want infested with it." Mama's eyes were twinkling, and those naughty little curls of hers were sneaking down on her forehead again.

"Mama, I think you mean infected," Lori corrected her, casting a worried glance at Jo.

"I know what she means," Jo answered, laughing," but here we call it auburn, not red, and people really envy all of us who are lucky enough to have it. I know all my friends admire my hair, especially the boys. I'd love to have breakfast with you, even though I've eaten once already. This fresh country air makes me ravenous, and that wonderful smell is too good to resist. It is nice to meet you too, Mr. Mueller."

"It is my pleasure," answered Papa,"and I would have said so sooner if I could have found a way to squeeze in a word. Let us now be seated and thank God for this special day."

"What special day is that?" asked Jo, looking puzzled. "Easter isn't until Sunday, is it? Or is the bunny coming early this year?"

"It is Good Friday, the day our Lord gave His life on the cross for all of us. It is fitting that we should remember." Papa began reading a passage from the Bible, then folded his hands and spoke a prayer.

Lori watched Jo out of the corner of her eye, and noticed that she listened solemnly to Papa's reading.

She folded her hands with them as Papa prayed. Lori wanted to hug this perceptive girl for realizing in an instant how important this day was to her and her parents, though it obviously was not important to Jo in her own life.

"So you too have a rest from school." Papa's voice was friendly. "What brings you to our farm country?"

"I love the country!" Jo's voice was eager and excited. "I feel so free in the great outdoors. I love exploring along the stream and in the meadow. Where I come from there are only houses, big buildings and stores. I have spent every Easter holiday here since I was five, and if I didn't love my parents so much I would just move in with Aunt Maud and Uncle Charlie .And it's so nice to have a neighbor my own age to explore with."

"How old are you, Jo? And why you have boy's name? The man owns store is Joe, but I not know it a girl's name too," Mama commented, looking rather puzzled.

Jo's laugh rang out in the kitchen. "That name has caused lots of arguments between my parents and me. You see, I am actually Joanna, but my heroine is Jo of the book "Little Women", so I decided to borrow her name. The teachers at school call me Joanna, but my friends all call me Jo. I am thirteen years old, and in the seventh grade. I started junior high this year. Mama told me to try to be a lady at school, but it is very hard, and very boring. I'd rather play football with the boys, but that is against the rules. There are so many rules it would make your head swim!" Jo tossed her head and waved her arms about, fork in hand.

"Will you help me with my science project?" Lori asked impulsively. "A friend and I are trying to identify some of the vegetation in this region. We could go exploring together with Harry. He's the one I'm doing the project with."

"A boyfriend?" asked Jo, but seeing Lori's shocked expression, quickly changed the subject. "Well, let's go, that is if your parents can spare you. Go comb your hair and put on your jeans."

"I do not wear jeans. Our religion teaches us that women should look like women, in dresses," said Lori quickly. "Mama, will you help me braid my hair?"

"That long hair must be an awful nuisance. Why don't you just cut it short so you wouldn't have to braid it every day? Just think how much simpler your life would be!" Jo pointed to her own flowing hair.

"We Mennonites believe that a woman's hair was given her by God, and that her hair is what makes her look like a woman. Lori's hair will stay as it is. And Lori cannot leave the house today. On this holy day she must think about more serious things. Since there is no church of our faith here we will have our own service. You are welcome to stay if you would like to." Although kindly said, there was unmistakable determination in Papa's voice.

"Thank you for asking," Jo answered. "But I think I will spend the day with my Aunt and Uncle. I'll be back tomorrow, if that's all right."

"You come back and share our midday meal? We have good Mennonite meal with Pflaumen Moos, Shinken, and eggs of pretty colors. Then Paska with coffee." Mama's eyes twinkled as she listed the strange sounding dishes in her native German.

"I'll take a chance on them, though I haven't the faintest idea what they are. I love surprises. I'll ask Aunt Maud and Uncle Charlie and if it's okay with them I'll be back." Jo grinned at Mama.

"We'll see you at noon then," called Lori as the door closed behind Jo. She loved the easy relationship that was developing between Mama and her new friend.

After Jo left, Mama, Papa, and Lori looked at one another and burst out laughing. "That Jo like fresh wind," Mama remarked. "Not shy, and makes us feel homely with her."

Lori smiled warmly at Mama. "I agree. But I think you mean she makes us feel at home with her, Mama. Homely is a word meaning ugly, or not pretty."

"Enough of all this talk about Jo. We must now be serious and think about Good Friday and what it means to us," said Papa sternly.

The rest of the morning was spent reading the Bible and praying. Jo arrived for the noon meal just as the Mueller's service had ended.

"I'm so glad you're back!" Lori put an arm around Jo. "Are you ready to eat real Mennonite food? We call it Mittag, and it is our big meal. I hope you like it."

Lori explained that Pflaumen Moos was a soup made of dried fruits including prunes and that Shinken was home smoked ham which one of their neighbors had given them. Jo ate it all, asking for more, and commented, "My, this is delicious, Mrs. Mueller. You are certainly a good cook."

"You fluttering me," laughed Mama, "so you can have some Paska."

"I think you mean flattering, Mama. But knowing you, you would give it to Jo whether she wanted it or not."

"The Paska is a sweet yeast bread which for us Mennonites always is used at Easter. We eat it only during this holy season," said Papa, who had been silent until now.

"It's as good as everything else," said Jo. "And thanks so much for having me."

"It is our happiness," answered Mama.

"Now that we have had our service would it be all right if Jo and I spent some time outdoors? I want to show her the goats." Lori looked at her Papa.

"It would be all right if you stay around here," Papa answered. "But do not leave our land."

The girls bounded out of the door almost before Papa had finished speaking. Jo headed for the brook behind the house when she noticed the goats. "What beautiful creatures!" she called out. "Do they have names?"

"Of course," Lori answered. "The brown and white one is Mandy. She's the one with all the spunk, always getting into trouble. She is afraid of nothing and will eat clothes or anything else we happen to leave around. Molly is kind of shy. Mandy reminds me of you, Jo, and Molly of myself. They are kind of like you and me. Even though they are so different, they love each other and stick together." The remark was almost a question.

"My Uncle thinks you are a wonderful girl, and I trust his judgment. And I think your mom is a real character. Your dad seems kind of strict, though. Can't you try to twist him around your finger just a little?"

"Papa is a fine man, Jo. But he sticks by what he believes in no matter what. I do not even try to oppose him. He is the head of our household, and our religion teaches us that he must be obeyed. Sometimes this is hard to do." Lori thought of her new clothes unworn in the box. "But I always have done just as he says."

"My dad is easy to manage," Jo commented. "He tries to be strict but I usually get my own way, except about spending the summer here. They think Easter holidays are long enough. But enough of that. Look at the brook over there! Let's go!" Jo bounded to the brook and began climbing one of the birch trees. "Come on up," she called to Lori. "You can see a lot from here."

Lori tried climbing the tree in her long dress, but made slow progress.

"I'll bring you a pair of jeans and we can hide them somewhere in the woods so your dad won't know," Jo suggested. "How about that?"

"I'm afraid that would be dishonest, and I couldn't do it. I'll manage." As she spoke she pulled her dress way up and reached a branch beside Jo.

The two girls surveyed the countryside from their vantage point, when Jo cried excitedly, "Look at the water bubbling right over there! Let's get down and see what's going on."

They decided that it must be a spring, for the water was squirting up right out of the bottom of the brook. "You know, Jo, when the weather gets hot we can use this as an icebox to keep our milk, cheese and butter cold. We could put them in jars and hang them from that tree branch right there. I can't wait to tell Mama. But Jo, look at this!" Lori held up a hard black object with a sharp point. "What do you suppose that is?"

"Why, I think that's an old Indian arrow head. I'll have to ask Uncle Charlie to be sure. He has found quite a few Indian artifacts on his land. Isn't it exciting to think that years ago there were Indians right where we are standing now?"

The rest of the afternoon was spent looking for more evidence of Indians until they heard Mama's voice calling them. "Lori and Jo, it is time for evening reading."

"I'll see you tomorrow," Jo said, giving Lori a hug. "Say goodbye to your Mama for me. It's been a wonderful day."

As Lori said goodbye she felt a surge of happiness and well being. It would be wonderful to spend the next little while with her new friend Jo. She decided not to think about school at all, but to spend the coming days as though they would last forever.

Eight

The days that followed were happy and busy ones for Lori. She and Jo spent all the time they could together, exploring the countryside, talking to Mama, Papa, Uncle Charlie, and Aunt Maud, and sharing confidences.

The weather was in their favor since this year April was sunny and mild. Spring was everywhere, and the girls could see its progress.

Jo's boundless energy was contagious, and Lori was willing to agree to all Jo's escapades and ideas. Her cheeks bloomed like the flowers around her, her eyes sparkled, and her feet hardly seemed to touch the ground.

"Our Lorchen very happy," Lori heard Mama saying to Papa one morning as she was dressing for breakfast. "I not seen her like that for much time."

"Ja, it is good to see," Papa answered. "I have worried about her."

"Good morning," Lori answered gaily as she entered the kitchen. "Isn't it just the most beautiful day? Must you work somewhere today, Papa?"

"I promised Mr. Manual I would help him dig up his garden," Papa answered, smiling fondly at his daughter. "Planting time is almost here. He will then help me dig up more garden space so we can add corn, potatoes, and other vegetables to my peas when it is warm enough. What will you do today?"

"Jo and I are going to look for more plants for my science project. I am pressing a sample of everything we find in this old Eaton's catalog Uncle Charlie gave us. Then I'll be able to identify everything from Miss Kent's book at school. I had no idea there were so many kinds of plants here. This is a much bigger project than I realized."

"And it is much fun, no?" Mama smiled warmly. "That Jo is right to help you. I never seen any girl with so much zoomph."

"You must mean oomph, although that is what is called slang. Energy would be a better word. But your English is really improving, Mama. You will be a real Canadian in no time," Lori teased.

"Never altogether," Mama answered. "I love this land, but sometimes I lonely for my beautiful Ukraine and the little Dorf where I grew up. I still hear Dneiper River. I shut my eyes I see school where my Papa teached. And Russian makes more sense than all mixed up English. But I have my family and new home that safe so I be happy here." Her wistful look was soon replaced by her sunny smile.

After breakfast Jo and Lori followed the brook through the fields and thickets. They carried a pail in which they placed the samples of vegetation they were collecting, making certain they did not miss even one precious plant.

"Since you are working on this project with Harry why don't we go to his place and include him in our search?" Jo asked. "I really would like to meet him."

Lori became very thoughtful. "That wouldn't be a good idea, Jo. Harry lives several miles away from here, I'm not exactly sure where. He walks by my house when he goes to school. And Papa does not approve of my keeping company with boys at my age. I'm afraid he wouldn't approve."

"Your father is living in a different world, Lori. He needs to adopt some Canadian ways. For your sake I hope he does. She turned and looked around. "How I love it here!" Jo's voice was exuberant. "Can you imagine living in a place where there are only houses and streets? I can go to the park, but then I've been there so often there are no surprises any more. I do have a bike which my parents let me ride around if I tell them exactly where I'm going. I brought it with me, by the way. You don't have one, do you, Lori?"

"No, but how I wish I did! We can not yet afford such a luxury. Perhaps by next spring when you come I'll have one, but first of all, Papa would have to get one. He walks everywhere, and he could save much time and energy with a bicycle to ride. Many people here use them instead of cars, you know. It's quite safe on these country roads."

"Somehow I cannot imagine your father riding a bike. He seems so stern and proper, as though he is afraid to try new things." Jo looked questioningly at Lori.

Lori was quick to come to his defense. "He is a very brave man, or he wouldn't have moved so far away from his own people. And he is stern and proper only where his religion is concerned. He and I had a falling out just before you came, and things have been a little strained." She told Jo about the box of clothes in Mama's bedroom.

"That's what I don't understand at all. Doesn't he realize that you would still be a fine person even in different clothes or wearing a pair of jeans? And your hair! How can you have the patience to be still while your mother braids that long hair every day?"

"Papa thinks my hair should be long. It is the way he was raised. And because he is such a fine man, and my religion teaches me to honor my parents, I do not cross him or argue with him. But I agree with you. Perhaps in time as he lives in this country he will change, though I'm afraid that will not happen overnight." There was a hopeless tone in Lori's voice.

"I just had a great idea! There's an old girl's bike in Uncle Charlie's woodshed that Aunt Maud used until her arthritis got so bad. I wonder if he would let us fix it up for you. Let's find out!" Already Jo was racing back towards the house and across the street to Mr. Manual's barn. Lori had a hard time keeping up with her, especially since she was carrying the pail with the plants in it.

"Uncle Charlie, Uncle Charlie!" Jo called even before she found him in his barn. "What are you going to do with that old bike in the woodshed? Would you let us fix it up for Lori since Aunt Maud can't use it any more? Then we'd both have a bike to ride and we could really explore this countryside. Oh, please say yes!" Jo stopped, trying to catch her breath.

"Slow down there, my dear. How can I answer you when I can't get a word in edgewise? Oh, hello there, Brown Eyes, I see you're having a hard time keeping up with this whirlwind here. Would you really like that bike? And if you had it how would you keep up with this dynamo?" His eyes looked fondly at Jo.

"I would love it, Uncle Charlie. But I'd have to ask Papa's permission first."

"Of course you would." Even as he was speaking Mr. Mueller was walking across the street to the Mueller farm. Jo was at his side in an instant.

"Oh, Mr. Mueller, Uncle Charlie wants to give Lori Aunt Maud's old bike. We could wash it, paint it, and repair it and then she would have a bike all her own and we could go riding together. Please say yes!"

Papa smiled at Jo's enthusiastic plea. "How could I say no to such a kind offer? I wonder whose idea that was." His eyes twinkled with amusement.

"Well, it was mine, but only because Uncle Charlie didn't think of it first. If he had he would have suggested it himself. Let's go, Lori, we have a lot of work to do." Jo was already half way to the woodshed.

Lori gave her Papa a hug. "I thank you for saying yes, Papa. And Uncle Charlie, I thank you for one of the nicest gifts I have ever had." Impulsively, she threw her arms around him and gave him a big hug, then ran after Jo who was already in the shed.

"Well, Jake, I wonder what you would do with a daughter like Jo." Lori heard Mr. Manual say as she entered the shed. She was glad she did not hear Papa's answer.

All the rest of that day the girls worked on the bicycle. They removed the dirt and rust and Uncle Charlie oiled it and made sure all the parts were tight and in working order.

When it was finished both girls uttered squeals of delight. Since it was a **girl's** bike and had no bar Lori would be able to ride it easily in spite of her long dress. "What are we waiting for? Let's go!" Jo called to Lori enthusiastically.

"I can't ride this bike, Jo! You know I have never owned one. Come and hold me up!" Lori called as she landed, bike and all, in the gravel on the road.

"I'm coming!" answered Jo, laughing. For the next few hours the girls practiced the art of bicycle riding. Lori, who learned quickly, was soon able to ride by herself, though she did fall down a few times.

"I think you are ready now." Jo finally decided. "Let's go clean it up and paint it now with the paint Uncle Charlie found. That way it can dry overnight. And tomorrow we'll cover the countryside."

"Tomorrow is Easter Sunday," Lori said regretfully. "And I will be spending that quietly with my family. But Monday morning will be fine. Papa's going home for supper now, so I'd better go too. I'll see you first thing Monday morning." Lori put down her bicycle, gave Jo a hug, and joined Papa who had left the field and was on his way home.

Jo waved goodbye to Papa and Lori, then waited for Uncle Charlie who had just finished mending the fences around the barn.

The Muellers spent a quiet Easter at home. After their service Lori settled down to read parts of the Bible. Try as she would she could not concentrate on her reading. The day seemed endless, and even her diary did not appeal to her. Why write, she thought, when there were so many exciting things to do in the coming week.

"I'm glad you have found a friend and are having a nice rest from school," Papa said before they went to bed. "But remember that Jo likes to do many things that you have never done. Be sure you think before you agree to all her ideas."

"I will be careful, Papa. But you really need not be afraid. Jo is kind of impulsive, but she knows the difference between right and wrong."

Papa said goodnight to Lori, agreeing, but adding that Jo's right and wrong did not always coincide with theirs.

The next morning the girls left the house right after breakfast and rode down the graveled road towards the school, over a mile away. "This is just heavenly!" Lori called to Jo riding ahead of her. "But please slow down, I'm still just learning to ride!"

The girls rode on at a more leisurely pace. When they passed the Chadsey store they saw a group of girls sitting on the porch. Susie, noticing them, walked down the steps and towards the road, followed by the three other girls.

"Hi, Lori. I see you have a new bike. It must be hard to ride in that long dress. Who's your friend?" Susie's voice had a curious ring to it.

"Susie Chadsey, this is Jo Manual from Vancouver. She's staying with her aunt and uncle for the Easter holidays." Lori also introduced Mary and the other two girls. They chatted for a while about the joy of holidays. Jo announced to everyone she loved the country and didn't care if she ever went home.

"Well, let's go, Lori. We've got a lot to see if we are going to get back before lunch." Jo was already on her bicycle.

"You must come visit me, Jo. I would love to show you my room and hear about the school you go to. You've got to tell me all about the city."

Jo got off her bike, looked straight at Susie, and said curtly, "I'm having too much fun exploring the countryside with Lori to sit in a bedroom, and I certainly don't want to talk about school on my holidays. It was nice meeting you girls." Her remark was obviously directed to the other three girls.

"Goodbye, Lori," Mary called after them. Lori turned around to wave and noticed the look of utter surprise on Susie's face.

"What a pill! I wouldn't visit that rude brat ever! Imagine her inviting me without you! How do you put up with her? And why do her friends let her get away with that rudeness?"

"I don't know, but most of them do. A couple of the girls have been trying to be friendly to me, but then Susie ignores them until they are under her spell again. I'm just too different for her taste, and she rules the roost."

"Too bad she lives out here in the country. She'd never get away with it in Vancouver, where there are many different races and peoples. She needs a lesson in manners and for some of the kids to take her down a peg or two. I bet she won't get away with it when she goes to school in Chilliwack next year. You ought to stand up to her, you know."

"I'm not too good at that yet," Lori commented. "But it looks like I'm going to have to learn. I can do it when she really makes me angry. I wish you went to school here. I could use a friend like you." The look Lori gave Jo was almost worshipful. "But let's not talk about her any more. We only have a week, and I want to enjoy every second of my holiday."

The girls spent the morning exploring the streams and the paths along the hills around the town. When they arrived back at the Manual's for lunch, they parked their bikes and entered the house with their arms around each other. Lori silently thanked God for sending her this wonderful friend.

Nine

Lori was sitting at the breakfast table and running her spoon through her puffed wheat, deep in thought. What a wonderful week it had been! She and Jo had ridden all over the countryside. Because all the farms were quite far apart they had not met any of the school children, although they had ridden by a mailbox with Toop on it. Harry, however, was nowhere to be seen.

"So you not eat this morning?" Mama asked. "You need all your energy if you ride bicycle all day long. Is Saturday already and your Jo go home tomorrow."

"I know, my dear Mama, that's what I was thinking about. It has all been so perfect, and tomorrow it will be over. I will have to go back to school, and my best friend will be far away. Can you understand how that makes me feel? Do you know how wonderful it has been to have a real and true friend, one who loves me just the way I am?"

"Of course I understand. Jo a very special person. Not happen often. But you can respond with her," Mama consoled.

Lori laughed heartily. Somehow Mama's English had lifted her mood. "I do believe you mean correspond, Mama. I will certainly do that. I plan to write to her every day. But now I'm off. Jo and I plan to ride to Chilliwack today, if that's all right with you. By the way, where's Papa? I forgot to tell him we were riding to Chilliwack. Do you suppose he would approve?"

"I told him," Mama said. "He not say no, so maybe that means yes, but he worries you run too much and not think of serious things. You know he likes you to read Bible every day and have time to talk to God. You not do that. Your mind been full of Jo."

"But I have been so grateful to God for sending me such a wonderful friend and I have thanked Him every day. I'm sure happiness is part of God's plan for me." Lori's whole face expressed joy.

"Do not worry. On Monday you have school, so today have happy day. Be home before dark," Mama kissed her daughter and Lori hurried out the door.

Lori and Jo rode the six miles to Chilliwack, browsed through every one of the half dozen shops and had lunch in the only cafe in town.

"Bless Uncle Charlie for treating us to lunch," Jo commented as they ate their tomato soup and toasted cheese sandwiches. "I bet you haven't eaten in a restaurant very often."

"I can't remember ever eating in one, Jo. Ever since I was born my parents have struggled just to keep us fed and clothed. And you know, I don't think they really like Canadian food. Our dishes are all so very different, and especially Papa likes things the way they have always been."

"I wonder if he'll ever change." Jo said, looking very thoughtful. "Your mom seems to adjust much more easily to new situations. Your father, forgive me for saying so, is inflexible and unbending. I can see trouble ahead for you if you ever oppose him."

"I know," Lori said. "I do agree with him about most things though. I believe very deeply in God and our religion. I just don't put as much emphasis on having a plain appearance. I believe it's what you are like inside that matters. God created this beautiful world and I think He would want us to be beautiful too. Papa thinks that outward appearance can make a person frivolous and lose sight of God, or at least divert their attention from Him. These religious ideas have been held by the Mennonites for centuries, and Papa says they have served them well."

"My parents don't even go to church very often," Jo commented. "They are still fine people. My dad is a lawyer and often defends people who can't afford to pay him. He really does a lot of good. I wonder if I can telephone them from here in Chilliwack. Uncle Charlie does not have a phone and I have missed them."

"I wondered if you had thought of your parents during your stay, since you never mentioned them." Lori said." I don't know how I'll get along without you. You are my first real friend in British Columbia; I mean one that's near my own age. Will you write to me?"

"Of course," Jo answered. "I'll want to know how your science project turns out. And what develops between you and Harry. Here's my address and telephone number. Put them in your pocket and keep them in a safe place."

Lori's face had turned quite red at the mention of Harry. "Thanks, Jo. You'll hear from me often. Nothing romantic will develop between Harry and me. For one thing, my Papa thinks I am far too young to have a boyfriend, and for another, Harry is two years older than I am and he wouldn't be interested in me like that. But we can be friends."

"That's a good place to start. He sounds as though he has enough sense to see what a super person you are, and you already know he thinks you're pretty smart. But let's go. I want to explore the old mountain road that winds along the Fraser River. We can go home that way."

The mountain road proved to be fascinating. The girls stopped many times to cut samples of new plants they saw.

"I'm so glad I left my shears in my bicycle carrier so that we can clip all these wonderful samples for your project," Jo said excitedly. "Look at this, Lori. If I'm right this is a dogwood tree. You'll have to check it out in your teacher's book next week."

The afternoon wore on as the girls kept laying their bikes by the side of the road to explore. Only a few cars passed them, and they saw only two farms. Often the road wound right next to the mountain, and the girls scrambled up its side. They drank water from a clear stream that flowed down the mountain by catching it in their cupped hands. They noticed squirrels scampering in the trees, enjoying the warmer weather.

"This is so much fun, but it's time to go home," Lori said reluctantly. "I promised Mama we'd be home before dark."

The girls went towards their bikes lying by the side of the road. Just as Jo picked up her bike Lori noticed a spring flower she had not seen before right by Jo's bike. She bent down to pick it just as Jo picked up her bike and started to move forward.

"Come on, Lori. If we have to go . . ."

"Wait! Wait!" Lori screamed. "My braid is caught!" Lori's head was bent as she pulled back from the moving bike. Her hair was stuck tightly in Jo's chain.

Jo stopped abruptly. "Wait," she said, carefully laying down her bike. "I'll have it out in a minute." She tried to move the chain, but it would not budge. She tried turning the pedal, but the pedal would not turn.

She looked at Lori and said, "That braid is really jammed in there, and I can't move it." Jo tugged and pulled, but only made matters worse.

"What can we do? How are we going to get home? You'd better try harder, Jo. If I move my head even a little it pulls so I could scream. For goodness sakes, do something!"

"I have that shears in the basket. I could cut it off, and then we could work at getting the hair out together. Or we could walk home. But you can't walk like this. Do you want to stay here while I use your bike to get help?"

"My Papa would be so angry if I came home with my hair cut off. You know that. He'd probably disown me. We'll have to get help." Lori sounded really desperate now.

"Okay, I'll go! There's a farmhouse about a half mile down. I'll try not to be too long. I hate to leave you like that." Jo was already on Lori's bike.

"Don't leave me here alone like this!" Lori screamed. "What would I do if a bear or something came along?"

Jo's voice was both pleading and convincing. "Are you trying to tell me that your Papa couldn't adjust to your hair being shorter? Surely even he would have to admit it isn't the end of the world." Jo's voice suddenly had a thoughtful ring to it. "I think this is a lucky stroke of fate. You can even call it God if you want to. You'll have short hair, something you've always wanted. And your Papa will survive. There really is nothing else we can do."

Lori, more uncomfortable by the minute, admitted to herself that what Jo said made sense. She had never done anything her Papa didn't approve of before, and the thought of doing this filled her with fear. But that fear wasn't nearly as great as the immediate one of being left while Jo rode for help.

While she was thinking Jo tried once more to get her braid out of the bike chain.

"Stop it, Jo, you're killing me! Okay, cut it off! Cut it shoulder length. If I'm going to be in trouble I might as well have it the length I want."

Lori gritted her teeth as Jo got the shears and began to cut. It took quite a few snips to get through the thick braid, which remained stuck in the bike chain. Finally Lori was free.

"Do the other one. Do it quickly before I have time to think!" Jo snipped at the other one until it too, was completely cut. Lori gasped, felt the ends of her hair, but said nothing.

Jo pulled a comb out of her pocket, combed Lori's hair, and then began trimming it with the shears. "I'm not a professional, but this will do. How great you look. I wish I had a mirror so you could see for yourself."

Lori could not speak. At first she felt only relief at being freed from the bike chain. Gradually the enormity of what she had done began to penetrate. Then came the fear; fear of what her Papa would say when he saw her. There was no escaping now.

Jo worked at the braid still caught in the chain. She had to cut it to pieces in order to get it all out. Finally the last strand was removed and the wheel turned once more. Lori picked up the other braid and put it into the pocket of her jacket.

"Let's go home," she said in a quiet but determined voice. "The sooner I face the music, the sooner it will be over with." Her face was white, her jaw set, and her eyes full of apprehension.

Jo walked over to Lori and put her arm around her friend. No words were necessary. The girls got on their bikes and rode home without a word. Lori's stomach was one big knot. She did not look about her, but followed Jo mechanically. Suddenly there it was, the path to her house.

"I'm coming in with you," said Jo as she turned into the path.

Lori straightened her shoulders, looked gratefully at Jo, and started up the path leading to her house. She placed her bicycle at the side of the house, felt her short hair, took a deep breath, and opened the door.

Ten

"Well, we're home," said Lori as she and Jo stepped into the kitchen.

Mama was busy at the stove, and said without turning, "Good, you here before dark. We have Rollkuchen for...."

Mama could not finish her sentence. Papa looked up from the book he was reading, threw it on the table, and shouted, "What is the meaning of this? What has happened to your braids? I cannot believe what I am seeing!" He got up from his chair and hurried towards Lori, his face ashen, his eyes blazing as he pointed to Lori's hair.

"Papa, I am so sorry. But my hair got caught in Jo's bike chain and we could not get it out, so we had to cut it. And once we had cut one braid it only made sense to cut the other one too." She looked pleadingly at Papa, whose face only became whiter. "I so hoped that you would understand," she added in a very quiet voice.

"Understand?" Papa's voice was shrill and angry. "I only understand that you have cut your hair without permission from me! And that you have made up some silly story about why you had to do it. I never thought that we would come to this, that you would not honor your mother and father as the commandments state very clearly." He went back to his chair and sat down, his expression grim, as he stared at Lori.

Before he could say anything else Jo walked towards him, stood directly before him and said, "Mr. Mueller, I did everything I could to get Lori's braid out of my bike chain. I would have had to leave her alone there on that mountain road while I went for help, and I didn't want to do that so I cut it off. Please try to understand. Lori feels very badly."

"What mountain road?" Mr. Mueller asked. "Lori did not have permission to ride down any mountain road. I'm afraid my daughter has not obeyed me. I cannot let you take the blame, Jo. I'm sure my daughter followed you down that road and gave you permission to cut her hair. But I will have to insist that she spend no more time with you since she cannot remember to obey her Papa. So I will have to ask you to leave and not return."

"Papa!" Lori cried. "You must not blame Jo for this! How can you send her away when she was only trying to help me? How can you send away my best friend?"

"I am sending her away to punish you, not her. It seems that you cannot remember the Lord, your God, when you have so much free time. Therefore I must put an end to it. Perhaps then you will spend your time thinking of what Mama and I have tried to teach you." Papa's voice was no longer shrill, but harsh and determined.

At the mention of Mama Lori turned around and ran to her. Even as Mama stretched out her arms Papa's voice rang out. "No, you do not go to your mother for comfort. You go to your room and think about what you have done. You will not be having supper with us tonight."

Lori stopped dead in her tracks and cast a pitiful look at Jo. Her friend stood in the center of the room, tears streaming down her face. She took a few steps toward Papa, then changed her mind and walked towards the door, opened it, and left without another word.

Lori felt as though all her joy had left with Jo. She went to her room, threw herself on her bed, and tried unsuccessfully to stifle the convulsive sobs that shook her whole body. Finally, she just gave in to her desperation, sobbing unrestrainedly until she could cry no more. Then she lay on her bed, just staring into space. She felt as though her whole world had collapsed. Uppermost in her mind was Papa's command that she not see Jo again. How could he do that, did he have no feelings for her? With a few words he had taken away her best friend, had deprived her of a precious treasure. The world which had been so perfect a few hours ago was suddenly bleak and cold.

Lori heard her parents talking in the kitchen. She heard Mama pleading with Papa to listen to Lori's story and forgive her. Papa replied that he would, of course, forgive her, but that it was his duty as the head of the household to discipline her so she would remember.

"I do not need you to interfere in this," she heard Papa say, "and I must insist that you abide by my decision."

After dark Papa asked Lori to join him and Mama in their evening prayer. Lori sat down at the table with them, her whole face swollen from crying. After reading a passage from the Bible and praying Papa addressed Lori. "It is necessary that you understand why it seems I have been so harsh and unfeeling. First of all, I do believe that your hair accidentally got caught in Jo's bicycle chain. Would you please tell me where it was caught, near the top or near the bottom?" Papa looked straight at Lori.

Lori did not look at her Papa when she answered him in a quiet voice, "Near the bottom."

"So that it would have been possible to cut it near the bottom, and save most of the braid. Is this correct?" Papa was still looking at her.

"Yes," Lori answered, her eyes still downcast.

"Then I am right to think you used this as an excuse to cut your hair short because that is what you really wanted? I want you to answer me." His voice was stern.

"Yes," answered Lori in a toneless voice. "But it did not occur to me at the time. I just wanted to get loose."

"This is exactly what I mean," Papa continued. "You were willing to lie to yourself to excuse what you did. You must see that this is how dishonesty begins."

At the mention of the word dishonesty Lori's downcast eyes suddenly turned straight to her Papa. There was anger in her voice as she said," Yes, Papa, I hate my hair long and I hate my clothes. I do not think God expects me to run around looking so ugly. I'm sure I will be just the same person with my hair short. I love you but I wish you would give me a little credit for being able to think for myself. I cannot think exactly like you do." The anger in her voice had been replaced by defiance.

Papa looked long and hard at his daughter. Then he said all too calmly, "As long as you live under my roof you will abide by my rules and my decisions. That is final. You will go to school each day but you will come directly home for one month. You will do your homework, read your Bible, and help your Mama. At the end of that time we will talk again. Good night now."

Lori went through the motions of saying good night to him, then went over to Mama and hugged her. Mama had not said one word through this whole conversation, but returned her hug warmly.

Once in her room Lori took her diary from the shelf and began writing.

Dear Diary:

I hardly know how to tell you about the events of the day. My hair is short at last but there is no joy in it. Papa has confined me to the house, where I must stay every day after school for one month. I will miss my meadow and all the places Jo and I discovered. But most of all I will miss my Jo. She is not even allowed to come say goodbye to me tomorrow, when she is leaving for Vancouver.

Right now I almost hate Papa. It is even hard for me to excuse his actions by saying he is trying to do what is right. Is it right to punish me so severely because I let Jo cut my hair? Is it right to take away the first true friend I ever had? I can see in Mama's eyes that she does not agree with Papa, but she will not defy him. Our religion teaches that the man is the undisputed head of the house, and Mama believes that.

I feel so lost, and alone. The thought of school makes me sad. Even the science project I worked so hard on has lost its appeal. Every sample of vegetation in that catalog will remind me of my Jo. I wonder if I am allowed to write to her.

Even God seems to have deserted me. Please, God, help Papa to see that he is being rigid and unfair. And help me get through the next few days.

Lori placed her diary back on the shelf, blew out the flame in the coal oil lamp and crawled wearily into bed. Totally exhausted, she fell asleep immediately.

The next day was Sunday, the last day before school began. Except for milking the goats, the Mueller's never worked on Sundays but conducted their own Mennonite service. Both breakfast and the service were unusually subdued. No unnecessary words were spoken, and even Mama lacked her usual sparkle.

Right after the service Lori heard a loud knock at the door. As Papa opened it she heard Uncle Charlie's familiar voice. "Jo wouldn't come with me to say goodbye, Jake. She seems to think that you have forbidden her to see Lori. She's mistaken, isn't she? Those two girls have become such good friends, it doesn't seem right not to let them say goodbye to one another."

"She is right. Lori has disobeyed me and cannot leave the house or see any friends for one month." Mr. Mueller did not even ask his neighbor to come in, but spoke to him at the door.

"For heaven's sakes, Jake, isn't that going a little too far? Jo was crying when she told me the whole story. She feels terrible. Lori has not committed a crime, and Jo had to help her out of a painful situation. And anyway, I see she looks right pretty with her hair short, at least from what I can see from here." Mr. Manual winked at Lori from the door.

Papa, angered by the wink, said curtly, "This problem is between my daughter and me. I will thank you to stay out of it. I will handle the situation as I see best. Now good day to you."

Before Mr. Manual left he called to Lori, "Jo says goodbye and wants you to know she loves you. She says she'll try to come for a few days this summer. Keep your chin up, Brown Eyes." Papa all but shut the door in Mr. Manual's face.

The uncomfortable silence continued for the rest of the day. Each of them had an open book before them and appeared to be reading.

Lori, with a library book on her lap, read each page several times. It's no use, she thought, I can't concentrate on a story or anything else.

She finally went to her cubbyhole and lay down on her bed, her eyes just staring into space. Jo was gone by now, she was sure. She imagined her sitting and looking out of the bus window, her sharp sparkling eyes drinking in the beauty of the countryside.

Just the thought of Jo left Lori with an empty, lonely feeling. And yet, she thought to herself, I haven't lost her. I know she will always be my friend.

Lori spent the rest of the afternoon lying on her bed, and remembering every moment of the wonderful days she had spent with Jo.

Finally the longest day of her life came to an end, and it was time to get ready for bed.

Eleven

Morning dawned all too soon. With a sinking feeling Lori realized that she would have to go back to school .She considered feigning illness but knew her Papa would never stand for that.

Lori looked over at Papa who was waiting for her to be seated so they could begin their morning devotions. He looked serious and grim as he was leafing through the Bible, finally finding a passage he wanted to read.

Without so much as a glance at Lori he read from Matthew. *"Do not lay up for yourselves treasures on earth, where moth and rust consume and where thieves break in and steal, but lay up for yourselves treasures in heaven, where neither moth nor rust consumes and where thieves do not break in and steal. For where your treasure is there will your heart be also."*

Next he folded his hands, motioning Lori and her Mama to do the same. "Heavenly Father, guide us all through this day, and help my daughter remember that she must not lay up treasures on earth, but keep her eyes on You and Your will. Let her grow strong again in Your ways, so that she will never again stray from them."

Breakfast was a totally silent meal. When Papa had eaten, he put on his coat and went outside to work in his garden.

Mama looked lovingly at Lori as she asked, "What would you like for lunch?"

Lori cast one pitiful glance at Mama. "It doesn't matter, anything will do. Mama, will he never forgive me? Does he not know that I wish none of this had happened? Oh Mama, how can I live in this house with him when he treats me like that? Can't you say something to make things better?"

"Your father is stubborn man. He not give up. You give him time. You know he be angry at me too if I say something. But is because he loves you, that I know."

Some love, Lori thought. She sighed, put on her coat, took her lunch pail, kissed her Mama, and walked slowly out of the door and down the path. Papa continued to hoe his peas without as much as a glance at her.

She walked slowly down the road, past the Manual's house, deep in thought. She saw no one there. Uncle Charlie must be in his barn. How she wished she could talk to him. She did not notice the robin perched saucily on a branch singing to the world.

"Wait for me! I've been trying to get your attention but you seem to be deep in thought." Harry, out of breath, caught up with her. His mouth flew open when she turned around. "Well, look at you! Your hair! It's very pretty that way. Why do you look so sad?"

Lori burst into tears, and amid sobs told Harry the whole story of her impromptu haircut and of the loss of her new friend, Jo. He listened attentively, and just let her talk. Finally he said, "I'm so sorry, Lori. But I think your Papa will come around. Just give him a little time. What about our science project? I looked for you during Easter holidays, but you had company, and I didn't want to intrude. Did you work on it?"

"Oh, yes, my friend Jo was very enthusiastic about it. We gathered and pressed many, many samples. But now that Papa has confined me to the house for one month I won't be able to work on it except at school. You probably should find a different partner." Lori looked at him, her eyes showing no enthusiasm.

"We've done most of the work, Lori. I have gathered many samples too. We'll tell Miss Kent the whole story, and perhaps she will let us use her books during recess and lunch to identify our samples. Lori Mueller, you are not a quitter. Cheer up. I know we'll work it out." Harry smiled encouragingly at her.

Lori gave him a grateful look. "Thanks. But I don't feel like my own person. I feel like a mouse locked in a cage. No matter what I say or do nothing changes. I dread meeting Susie and her friends, who are all going to make snide comments about my hair. Besides, it is very embarrassing to have to tell Miss Kent that I am grounded for a month, and why."

"If anyone will understand, she will," Harry commented. "She has helped me over many rough spots."

They neared the school, where children were already standing in line, Susie among them. As she turned around to talk to one of her friends, she spotted Lori and gasped. "Well, would you look at that!" she said in a loud voice. "Look at Lori's hair! I can't believe your father actually let you cut it! Maybe one of these days he'll let you shorten your dresses too, and then you'll look almost like everyone else."

"Your hair looks very nice, Lori." Mary said. Several of Susie's friends nodded in agreement.

Alice walked over to her and gave her a big hug, smiling as she did so. "It's good to see you," she said. "I have missed you so much. I wanted to come visit you but Papa wouldn't let me."

"Because I'm German?" Lori asked, suddenly realizing that Alice must have a hard time explaining to her father why she had a German friend. From what Alice had told her about him, she knew he was full of prejudice, and expressed it especially when he was drinking. "Thanks for being my friend anyway," she said, putting her arm around Alice.

"My goodness, short hair and a boyfriend," Susie continued in her jeering voice. "Does your father know you have a boyfriend? How does he feel about that? Did your friend from Vancouver have something to do with all of this? Miracles do happen, don't they? Now all you have to do is teach your mother proper English and you'll be fit to live in this country."

Harry, sensing that Lori was near tears, looked straight at Susie and said, "Why don't you leave her alone? Can't you find something better to do with your time than constantly tease her? You are being unkind and rude. It's high time you stopped, or even your friends will have had enough of all this unkind talk."

"The knight in shining armor comes to the lady's defense. In that case I had better stop. Anyway, the doors are open. Let's go, gang."

Miss Kent greeted Lori with a warm smile. "Your hair is very attractive that way," she said to her. "It really highlights your brown eyes."

At recess Lori and Harry stayed behind to talk to Miss Kent. Lori told her the whole story of the unfortunate haircut, and asked if she and Harry could work on their science project every noon because she could not leave the house for a month.

"That will be fine," Miss Kent said. "I'm sorry your father is so unhappy about your hair. But what's done is done, and I hope he will accept the situation in time." Seeing the pained expression on Lori's face, she added, "And if you ever need to talk, you know I'm here and willing to listen."

"Thank you so much, Miss Kent," Lori said gratefully.

Once on the playground Lori found Alice. They had much to talk about as they wandered arm in arm through the school yard. Each time Lori told the story of her hair she had to fight back the tears as she thought of Papa and his reaction to the whole thing. Each time she mentioned Jo's name she felt a deep sadness that she could not shake. The girls avoided the other students, and were surprised when the bell rang.

At noon she and Harry used Miss Kent's books to see if the specimens they had each gathered were listed. "A lot of the ones I found seem to be in this book. Let's each bring our samples tomorrow so we can check them." Harry said excitedly. Looking at Lori, he saw that she was turning the pages mechanically, showing no excitement, and taking notes on paper without comment.

He kept trying to get her interested. "Would you look at this, Lori? It's a whole page on salmon berries with their scientific name included. You know there are a lot of them in this region. And here are buttercups with their scientific name. The book tells you all the places where they can be found besides here on the west coast. They are usually places with similar climates. We are going to learn a lot by the time we finish this project."

"I guess we will," answered Lori Harry said nothing further, realizing that nothing could change Lori's mood.

At last the long, long day was over. Lori walked home alone, a faraway look in her eye. At the Manuals she stopped to talk to Uncle Charlie, who was near the road. "Would it help if I talked to your Papa?" he asked. "Jo feels so terrible about all this. She wonders if she should write you a letter or not."

"I thank you for trying to help, Uncle Charlie, but there's no use talking to Papa. It would probably make matters worse. As far as a letter is concerned, I think Papa would object even to that. In any case, I do not intend to push him further. I am in enough trouble now. I'd better go. Good bye, Uncle Charlie."

Mama was waiting for her in the kitchen. "And you have good day, my Lorchen? Was it good to be back in school?"

"It was dreadful, Mama. All I could think of was how much I hated to come home, and it's the first time I have ever felt that way. Do you know, Mama, it's as though there's a big stone in my stomach, and no matter how I try it won't go away. There is nothing I feel like doing except riding my bike as fast as I can. And you know I can't do that. So I'll just go to my room and lie down on my bed. If you need me for anything, please call."

Lori stretched out on her bed and thought. She could see the aspen trees through her window. It would help so much if she could go to her meadow, lie down on her stomach, and watch God's wonderful world burst into bloom. But even God seemed to have forgotten her. She tried to pray, but could not put her thoughts into words. She tried writing in her journal, but the pen would not move. Even tears, which were usually so healing, would not come.

Dry eyed and solemn she went to the table when Mama called her.

Twelve

Time dragged slowly for Lori as she went to school every day, then came directly home to stay in her room. Each night, as she noticed the new leaves and blossoms fairly growing before her very eyes, a deep sadness overcame her. April must be exceptionally warm this year, she thought, as she shed her warm coat on the way home at the end of her first week of involuntary confinement. How she longed to romp in her meadow, or follow the brook where frogs were croaking a glad chorus to spring. There must be eggs in the brook by now that would soon become tadpoles.

Three more weeks of this seemed like an eternity to her. She hadn't even dared stop to greet Molly and Mandy, the goats. Perhaps, when her confinement was over, they would have forgotten her.

She had spoken to Uncle Charlie only once. He had a big smile on his face as he handed her an envelope with her name on it. "This came tucked into the letter Jo wrote us. She decided to send it to us to save you further trouble with your father."

Lori's eyes lit up. "Oh, I thank you, Uncle Charlie. I'll take it home and read it in my bedroom." She walked away quickly, knowing that if she stayed to talk she would begin to cry.

That evening in the privacy of her bedroom she read the letter. Jo told her how unfair she thought her father was, and how sorry she was about the whole unfortunate episode. "Remember I will always be your friend," she ended. "Somehow this will pass and we will explore the countryside together again. I'm trying to convince my parents to let me spend part of my summer holidays with Aunt Maud and Uncle Charlie. I love you always, Jo."

Summer is a long way off, thought Lori. Right now it seems like an eternity. But that night she dreamt about Jo and the summer holidays.

As the week progressed she became even more despondent. Papa was busy working on the neighboring farms, and Mama went to the Chadseys several times a week. Once when Mama didn't feel well and could not go to work she had asked Lori to deliver a loaf of homemade bread to the Chadseys on her way to school.

"Oh, you must be the Mueller girl," Mr. Chadsey had said when she handed him the bread. "How thoughtful of your mother to send this. Let me call my wife. I would like you to meet her."

Mrs. Chadsey proved to be as pleasant as her husband. "Come into the kitchen where Susie is just finishing her breakfast. It is Lori, isn't it? The two of you can walk to school together."

Lori followed Mrs. Chadsey into the kitchen, where Susie was just getting up from the table. "What are you doing here?" she had said to Lori. "I don't remember asking you to call for me."

"Lori dropped some bread by because her mother is sick and cannot come today." Mrs. Chadsey was obviously embarrassed by Susie's sharp remark but made no comment to her daughter. Susie put on her sweater, said goodbye to her parents, and opened the door.

"Be sure you come again," Mrs. Chadsey said as Lori followed Susie out of the door."

"Yes, do," said Mr. Chadsey. "We think a lot of your mother and would like to get to know you too."

"My parents are too kind for their own good," Susie had remarked as they walked towards school. "They do favors and give credit to far too many people." Then, when she saw Mary just ahead of them, called "Wait, Mary," and ran off, leaving Lori behind.

At home in the days that followed, Mama was pleasant as ever, but Papa scarcely spoke to her, except to remind her to read her Bible. He seemed to Lori like a stranger whom she had never known. How could their warm relationship be destroyed by one haircut, she wondered. Papa came home late every evening, had dinner with them, read a chapter from the Bible, prayed, and then went to bed. Not once in all this time had he called her Lorchen, patted her head, or asked her how school was.

Lori noticed that although Mama tried to be pleasant her usual gay mood was gone. She always asked Lori about her day, but seemed unusually subdued. Her parents had little to say to one another. The whole atmosphere in the house was one of tension and uneasiness.

She thought about school. Harry had tried in vain to interest her in their project. He had accused her of being a quitter, had dared her to make the best of this situation, and had finally given up and begun mounting and labeling the samples with little help from her.

The weekend proved to be a nightmare to Lori. On Saturday she helped Mama clean the house and do the baking without as much as a word. Finally

Mama stopped what she was doing, looked long and intently at Lori, and said, "Sit down here beside me, my Lorchen. I want talk."

Lori obeyed as the two sat on the bench at the kitchen table. "We not go on like this," Mama said sternly. "It seem a funeral in here. Why can't you smile at Papa like you do before? He loves you. One smile you be friends again. This I know. Somebody must move first, somebody must give up stubborn. You two worser than goats outside."

Even Mama's English did not bring a smile to Lori's lips. With a deep sigh she said, "Then let him do it. You know, Mama, that I have been punished over and over for what I did. If Papa wants to live this way, so can I."

"And make me miserable too. Such piggish people I never seen. The Bible says we forgive, and Papa needs be forgiven."

"Then let him start by forgiving me. I cannot put my hair back on my head." Tears welling in her eyes, Lori bounded into her own bedroom.

Sunday was even worse. Papa was at home all day, and since Sunday was the Lord's Day no one worked. In her room after breakfast, Lori heard Mama say, "Why can't you talk to own daughter? You stubborn too long. She so sad. Makes me sad."

Lori did not hear Papa answer, but heard him stomp outside.

On Monday Miss Kent asked Lori to stay in at recess because she wanted to talk to her. "I'm very worried about you, Lori," Miss Kent began. "You have been in a world of your own all week. You look very sad and your work has been average at best. Harry tells me you have no enthusiasm for your science project and it is due at the end of next week. I had much hope for that project, and thought you and Harry would be eligible for the Provincial Science Fair. You are really letting him down, you know. He came to me only because he didn't know where to turn."

Lori burst into a flood of tears, sobbing uncontrollably, unable to answer her beloved teacher. How could she explain to Miss Kent that her relationship with Papa had turned her world into a dismal place, and that she felt as though there was a heavy stone in her stomach?

Miss Kent put an arm around Lori, saying quietly, "Tell me about it. Perhaps I can help."

"No one can help," Lori said tonelessly when she was finally able to speak. "Papa is angry because I cut my hair. I do not see how I can make up for it or change it. I have tried, but I cannot seem to concentrate on anything." Her tear stained eyes looked beseechingly at Miss Kent.

"There must be more to it than that," Miss Kent said musingly." He must feel that you are straying away from your religion and all the things he taught you. I know this is not the case, that you are a fine and honest girl. I'm sure in time he will come to see that too. You know, it's very hard for first generation children to grow up in a country new to their parents. But I'm sure you will manage to bridge this gap. From what I know of your father I know that he cares a great deal for you. Right now he feels very threatened by this culture new to him. And there are as yet no other Mennonites here to support him."

"I thank you so much for understanding," Lori said quietly, looking up at her teacher with eyes full of love." I will try to be happier and keep my mind on my schoolwork and our project. Harry has been so understanding, I hate to let him down."

At lunch time Lori worked on the project with feverish energy, trying her best to show some enthusiasm. Harry was much relieved. "Now we are getting somewhere. I'm sure we will be ready by the end of next week. Maybe we'll even be famous if our project gets picked for the Provincial Fair in Vancouver."

The word Vancouver sent hope into Lori's heart. That's where Jo lived and perhaps by some miracle she would be able to see her friend. For the next few days she worked without any break, intent on the project. No matter what, she decided, she would not disappoint either Harry or Miss Kent.

On Wednesday when Papa came home he carried the mail which had been delivered to the mailbox in his hand. He spoke to his daughter in a kindly voice. "Good evening, Lorchen. I hope you have had a good day."

Lori's heart skipped a beat. That sounded much more like Papa, and she looked up at him and smiled. "Yes, Papa, I did. Our science project is going very well. I hope your day was good as well."

Papa did not answer, but was intently reading one of the letters he had received in the mail. His face became sterner and sterner, his eyes blazed as he glared at Lori, saying, "What is the meaning of this?" and handed her the letter.

Lori looked at the letter. Her face became pale as she read:

Dear Mr. and Mrs. Mueller,

Ever since Lori has returned from her Easter Holidays she has been very preoccupied. I am very concerned about her declining work at school. After talking to her I feel it is essential that we have a conference as soon as possible. Would it be possible for you and Mrs. Mueller to meet with me after school on Thursday? I am looking forward to talking with you.

Sincerely,

Miss Kent

"And what is the meaning of this?" Papa repeated in an ominous voice. "I thought you just told me that everything was going well. Have you now begun to lie to your papa? Miss Kent writes that you are not doing your work as you should."

"I wasn't," Lori answered, fear in her voice. "But Miss Kent talked to me on Monday, and I have been trying since then. She must have written this letter before she could see that. I promise you, Papa, that I will do my best from now on."

"You surely will!" Papa answered in an angry voice. "We had trouble enough before but this letter shows me that you have gone too far and not obeyed me again. Go to your room. I do not wish to see you again tonight."

Lori put the letter on the table and went to her room. She sat there, just staring into space. She was sure Miss Kent meant well, and was trying to help her. But Papa! He seemed to think the worst of her, not accepting her explanation about anything. She hated to think of what he would say to her teacher tomorrow. Somehow this was a situation she could not face. There had to be a way out! The very thought of Papa telling Miss Kent how he felt about her act of defiance, as he saw it, sent chills up and down her spine.

Perhaps Miss Kent, in her quiet way, could help him see that she was really the same girl she had always been, even with short hair, and that it was his attitude that made her so unhappy. Sadly she put that idea aside. It would not work. If Papa's love for her could not break down this barrier, how would a few words from Miss Kent?

That night, as she lay wide awake in bed, an idea began forming in her mind. As the hours passed a definite way out of the situation emerged.

She got out of bed, found Jo's address, and began going over every detail of what she intended to do. Dawn was breaking when she fell asleep, her plan ready to be put into operation.

Thirteen

"It is time now to get up!" Lori heard Mama calling all too soon. "Come and eat with us breakfast."

Was the night really over? She tried to wake up. Then she remembered last night and her plan. Quickly she got out of bed, put on her school clothes, pulled a brush through her short hair, and went into the kitchen.

After the Bible reading and prayer, Papa said in a quiet but determined voice, "Wait for us in your classroom, Lori. Mama and I will be there to talk to your teacher. I want that you should be there too." He got up, took his lunch box, and was out of the door before Lori could answer him.

"Now something for your lunch," Mama said, "What you like to have? I can give you today cookies, apples and a sandwich of jelly and peanut butter."

"Thanks, Mama. You have much to do. I can make my own lunch today. I see the apples and cookies on the shelf."

While Mama was in the bedroom making the beds Lori quickly sliced four large pieces of bread, made two sandwiches and put them in a paper sack. She had added six cookies and two apples when Mama reappeared in the kitchen. She tried to put her coat over the lunch but Mama saw it.

"My goodness, lunch very big," Mama remarked. "Maybe you feel better `we talk to your teacher, no? Maybe we can make a few things straight, and everything be better. Why you not take the lunch pail as always? You want to eat dry bread?"

"I'd rather just take this paper sack if it is all right with you. I promised Alice I would bring her a sandwich of your homemade bread one of these days, so today's the day. And I might as well share cookies and an apple with her." Lori tried to appear calm, but her stomach was churning.

"That Alice is good friend, no?" Mama said. "When you not stay in the house no more maybe you bring her to meet with us."

"Maybe, if her father will let her come. He doesn't approve of Germans." Lori commented.

"He will when he meet us," Mama answered.

Lori ignored Mama's remark. She wanted to leave as soon as possible. Not telling her mother the truth about the lunch felt very uncomfortable. A full fifteen minutes earlier than usual she was out of the house. A check of her bicycle on the way out assured her that the tires were full of air.

Lori walked slowly, not wanting to arrive at school too early. Thank goodness Mama had not noticed that she was wearing her winter coat in spite of the warm spring weather. Her hand slid into her pocket. Jo's address was still there, just where she had placed it last night. If only everything would go as planned. She tried to ignore the anxious feeling that wanted to envelop her, and walked faster.

Because it was early Lori sat on one of the swings, just thinking. She knew that it was important to remain cool and natural so that no one would suspect her plan. Soon a line of children was forming at the door, and she walked quietly over to join them. No one spoke to her this morning, and once inside she placed her big lunch on the shelf. Miss Kent called to her then, and in a quiet voice said, "Are your parents coming in for a conference today, Lori?"

"Yes, they are," she answered in a barely audible voice, not looking at her teacher.

"I wrote the letter they received right after our talk," Miss Kent continued. "You have really tried to do your best since then, but I can't help feeling that your heart is not in it, and that talking to your parents might make things easier. Don't you think so?"

"Perhaps," Lori said in a noncommittal voice and went to her seat without looking up.

At lunch time Lori did not share her lunch with Alice but left the remaining sandwich, cookies and apple in the paper sack. While the children were filing out to play she stuffed them into her coat pocket.

For the rest of the lunch hour she worked feverishly on her science project, while talking uninterruptedly to Harry. "We are done with the classifying, and can now start mounting these samples in their proper order on the white cardboard, don't you think?" she asked Harry as she was already working on the first one.

"How about putting them right side up?" Harry remarked dryly. "Lori, you are acting like someone meeting a deadline a half hour from now. What is the matter with you? We still have over a week, you know."

"I want to get it done," she said almost vehemently. "I think we'll need quite a few pages for the trees, don't you?"

Before Harry could answer the bell rang signaling the end of the lunch hour, and they put their samples on the back table.

When afternoon recess finally arrived Lori put on her coat, the lunch sack bulging in her pocket. "I don't think you'll need that coat," Alice, who was waiting for her, commented. "I think your sweater will do."

Without answering Lori walked outside in her heavy coat. She turned to Alice. "I don't feel well," she said. "I'm going home. Please tell Miss Kent where I have gone."

"You can't just walk out of here!" Alice called after her. "You have to get the teacher's permission." But Lori was already on the road and ignored Alice's remark.

She walked home as fast as she could, frequently looking behind her to make sure no one from school was following her to bring her back. When she reached home she ran to the shed and grabbed her bicycle. How lucky that neither Mama nor Papa had arrived home yet. Quickly she took her lunch out of her pocket, put it in the carrier, and headed down the road.

It wouldn't be safe to go back the way she had come, Lori reasoned, since that road passed the Chadsey store and the school. There was another dirt road leading in the opposite direction that led to the main highway.

She decided to take that road since few people used it and she wasn't likely to be seen.

The road was far longer than Lori remembered, and the riding was rough. Finally, after what seemed an eternity, the highway appeared. A wooden sign with an arrow on it pointed in the direction of Vancouver. She bicycled at the edge of the road to avoid the few cars that passed her.

Since she did not have a watch she bicycled for what seemed to her to be hours. She had no idea how far Vancouver was from where she lived, but Mr. Chadsey went there often to get supplies for his store, so it couldn't be too far. Her legs ached and she was incredibly thirsty, but she had to go on.

Surely she would be able to reach Vancouver before dark, find a telephone and call Jo. Lori had never used a telephone, but perhaps someone would be there to help her. Stores very often had telephones. In any case, it was important to reach Vancouver first.

But why was it getting so dark already? Lori looked up and saw very dark clouds in the western sky. They seemed to be moving towards her at a rapid pace. Then she noticed the trees beginning to sway and felt the wind on her face. It was getting more and more difficult to pedal her bicycle.

Suddenly it began to storm, and the wind picked up. Great torrents of rain pelted down on her, driven by the April wind. The rain dashed harshly against her face. In a matter of minutes she was completely drenched.

Fear overcame her as she realized she could no longer keep the bicycle on the road. She looked around for some shelter but saw only a lone birch by the side of the highway. Shivering and icy cold she laid her bicycle down under the tree, and looked for a dry place to sit. The grass was as wet as everything around her, and the strong wind whistling through the branches sounded ominous and eerie.

In tears now, Lori groped for her lunch in the bicycle carrier. It was totally drenched, the paper sack torn and the sandwich and cookies soaked through and through. Only the apple was unharmed. She grabbed it, hoping its juice would help quench her thirst.

Lori, shivering now, sat down on the wet grass and took a bite of the apple. The trees in the distance were swaying violently now, the rain, blown by the wind, was pelting her face. It felt as though someone was poking pins into her. Another wave of fear gripped her. What was she to do? There was no farmhouse in sight, only the whistling sound of the driving wind, and the clatter of the piercing rain on the leaves of the tree.

Still thirsty, she stuck out her tongue to try to catch some of the rain water. Then she saw a big puddle that had formed right next to the tree. Lori lay down on her stomach and drank some of the water from the puddle. It did help her thirst, but as she tried to get up her feet gave way beneath her and she landed right in the water.

"Papa, Papa!" she cried out in a voice pained by terror. "Oh God, please help me! I know I was wrong to run away. Please send someone to find me. It is getting so dark and I am so very very cold!" She tried to fold her hands in prayer, but they were shaking so hard and her fingers were so cold she could not do so.

She pulled her knees up under her wet coat, leaned against the trunk of the tree, and kept praying. "Forgive me, Papa!" she cried out loud again. "Forgive me, God, and help me! Oh, help me!"

The whistle of the wind was her only answer. There were no cars or trucks on the road, only water beginning to collect everywhere. Oh, why had she left without writing a note? Why had she not told her parents in a note what she was planning to do, that her whole world had been destroyed by the haircut and the conference? Perhaps, if he had realized the depth of her unhappiness, Papa would have listened to her after all. Perhaps Miss Kent would have said something that would have made him understand. A deep longing for the loving arms of her Papa overcame her. "Papa, I am still your Lorchen, in spite of everything," she whispered through the wind. "Right now I want nothing more than just to see you. I want to tell you how I have missed you and how sorry I am that I turned away from you because I thought you wrong. Oh, Papa, please find me! Can you hear me calling?"

Completely exhausted and chilled to the bone, Lori finally lay down in the wet grass under the tree. She must have fallen asleep because it seemed to her that her Papa was bending over her and saying "Oh my Lorchen, I am so glad I found you."

Fourteen

"Lori Mueller! Wake up! Wake up! Please open your eyes and speak to me!" The sound seemed to be coming from far away. Lori heard it again and again. She tried to open her eyes, but the lids felt so incredibly heavy. She tried to move, but her body would not respond.

She felt strong arms lift her and carry her. "We'll have to get you out of these drenched clothes," she heard a man's voice say as she felt herself laid down somewhere. "Papa," she murmured, as she felt someone tugging at her jacket, and then pulling at her clothes.

"No, I am not your Papa, but do not be afraid. I am Joe Chadsey, Susie's father. I was coming home from Vancouver with a load of supplies for the store and I saw you lying here. You are chilled to the bone; all your clothes are drenched through and through. We must get them off immediately. Can you help me just a little bit? I have no other clothes here but I thought we'd wrap you in this warm car blanket until I can get you home."

"Mr. Chadsey?" Lori said in a weak voice. She was finally able to open her eyes and saw Susie's father looking down at her.

"I-I I'm sooo cold," Lori murmured. She saw that they were in the front of a truck, and that Mr. Chadsey was struggling with her dress. She tried to help him get it off, but her body would not respond.

"There, it's off. Now we'll put this blanket around you, and drive like mad. We are still about twenty miles away from home. The rain has died down but the wind is still blowing. Do your parents know where you are, Lori?"

At the mention of her parents Lori remembered. They were going to have a conference with her teacher, something she did not think she could face. She remembered deciding to leave home and go to Vancouver to find Jo. Then she remembered the rain and the wind, and how cold and wet she had been. How stupidly she had acted! Her parents must be beside themselves with worry not knowing where she was in that storm! How lucky for her that Mr. Chadsey had gone to Vancouver, or no one might have found her.

"No," she finally answered in a monotone. "I was going to Jo's in Vancouver."

"You just rest and don't try to explain," Mr. Chadsey said in a kind, gentle voice. "The important thing is to get you home and into some dry clothes. Your parents are probably frantic by now. Let me put your bicycle in the back of the truck."

Lori heard him open the back of the truck and rummage around in it. "Now we're all set," he said as he returned to the front of the truck and started the motor. "Are you feeling any warmer?"

"Just a little," Lori answered. "But my whole body feels stiff."

"Small wonder," Mr. Chadsey answered. "It is seven o'clock at night so you must have been there for hours. We've had one of the worst wind and rain storms I remember in these parts. These spring winds come up suddenly and bring much rain with them when they do."

Lori hardly heard him, she was just grateful to be in a dry place. She thought about her own warm bed, and the little house she shared with her parents. Right now it seemed like a palace to her. Her one desire was to be safe in those four walls once more. How could she have left them because of a conference? How could she have been so angry at Papa that she actually took her bicycle and left. Right now it seemed like an incredibly stupid thing to have done.

Mr. Chadsey said nothing else for the rest of the way. Lori was grateful she did not have to talk. She could hear the wind whistling against the truck, and snuggled deeper into her blanket. She dozed from time to time, waking with a start each time and wondering where she was.

They must be getting close to home. Lori's heart began beating faster. What would her reception be? Would they be angry or relieved? Somehow it hardly mattered as long as she was home once more. She tried to look out of the window of the truck but the blanket held her like a papoose.

"There's someone in the middle of the road waving his arms to stop us!" Mr. Chadsey called to Lori. The truck skidded, and then stopped, as Lori craned her neck to peer out of the window.

There, in the middle of the road was a man frantically waving his arms. As Mr. Chadsey rolled down the window, she heard the man call, "Would you help me please! My daughter Lori is missing. I have just been to the store to call the police, but the phone is not working. I must get to Chilliwack to tell the police so they can look for my daughter!"

"Here I am, Papa! I'm right here in Mr. Chadsey's truck! I'm sooo glad to see you!" Lori's voice was shaking with emotion.

Suddenly the door of the truck was flung open and Papa had his arms around her. "My Lorchen, my Lorchen," was all he could say. Lori burst into tears and sobbed uncontrollably as she tried in vain to get her arms out from under the blanket. "Papa, my Papa," she finally managed to murmur.

"Why don't you sit down next to your daughter?" Mr. Chadsey said, his voice shaking with emotion. "I found her asleep under a birch tree next to the highway on my way home from Vancouver. She was totally drenched and cold to the bone. I'm sure she'll tell you all about it later." He turned the corner. "This is your road. We are almost home."

Lori snuggled against Papa. "Oh Papa, I am so sorry!" she began.

"Do not talk now," Papa said, his face still white and strained. "First we must thank God that you are safe, and then we must hurry to your Mama and Mr. Manual. They are sick with worry about you. Now fold your hands under that blanket. God, we thank Thee for bringing our Lorchen safely home. Help me to find the right way to deal with all our problems."

"Here's your path." Mr. Chadsey interrupted. "I cannot drive in but I will carry Lori to the house."

Before he could do so Mama, seeing the lights of the truck, came running up the path. She opened the door of the truck and began to cry when she saw Lori snuggled against Papa. "Oh my Lorchen, oh my Lorchen." she cried. "Thanks be to God you are here. We so afraid. We not know what we to do or where look to find you. You be found, you be found! Praise be to God." She reached across Papa to hug her daughter, then called out of the truck window, "She here, Mr. Manual, our Lori right here!"

"I just want to go home, to my own room," Lori finally managed to say through her sobs. "I want to curl up in my bed and pull the featherbed over me. I'm so cold. Please carry me back to my bedroom, Papa. I want to sleep and sleep and sleep."

Mama and Papa looked at each other knowingly. Mr. Chadsey just stood there behind Mama, a solemn look on his face.

Fear gripped Lori again. What was the matter? Her parents were so glad to see her; could Papa still not forgive her or understand?

Finally Papa said, "Something has happened, Lori. The strong wind blew a big cottonwood tree right on our house, and the roof has been broken. The rain came in, and everything is wet. The tree is right now lying in the middle of our kitchen. We cannot get into the bedrooms even if we wish. We have no place to sleep. We did not know what to do when we could not find you, so we have done nothing about the house. The only important thing was to find you. We looked everywhere outside, so we were not in the house when the tree fell. While we searched we kept praying that God would take care of you and bring you home to us. As you can see, He answered our prayer."

Lori burst into tears again. "How awful!" she sobbed. "You had to worry about me, and you lost our house! Our comfortable, homey house." Lori had quite forgotten that she had been ashamed of it when Susie visited them.

"I know what to do," Mr. Manual remarked as he came up to the truck. "We have a spare room which we keep just for Jo. It happens to have a double bed so her parents have a place to sleep when they come. There is also a cot we set up for Jo when her parents are here. Of course you will all come home with me. You, Brown Eyes, can wear some of the clothes Jo forgot here. Goodness knows she would not mind"

"You are too kind, Mr. Manual. But we could not do that." Mr.Mueller looked dejectedly at his wife. "Perhaps we could put the goats outside and live in their shed until we can build another house. Your wife Maud is not too well and we would be much trouble."

"Living in the goat shed is the most ridiculous thing I have ever heard. And I know that Maud would not mind if you stayed with us. She knows how hard you work, Mrs. Mueller, and you could do cooking and cleaning. Maud already loves our Brown Eyes. As far as I'm concerned, it's settled. You will stay with us. How do you think Jo would feel if our neighbors lived in a goat shed while her room stood empty?" He patted Lori's head. "We've got to get this girl into warm clothes and into bed or she'll catch her death of cold."

"Just get into the front of the truck, Mrs. Mueller," Mr. Chadsey then suggested. "Your husband can hold Lori on his lap, while Mr. Manual walks the short distance."

The Muellers argued no more, but got gratefully into the truck. Papa held his daughter on his lap and gently stroked her hair. The warmth of Papa's hand felt better than even the blanket had. She snuggled up to him as best she could.

"I'm so sorry, Papa," Lori began." I didn't know how much I loved you and Mama until I was freezing under that tree in the wind and the rain. I kept wishing that I had left you a note so you would know where to look. Or that I had never left at all," she added in a remorseful voice.

"Let us not say more now," Papa interrupted her. "I did not know either how stubborn I had been, how without forgiveness until the wind blew and we could not find you. We will talk all about it tomorrow." He continued to stroke his daughter's hair, a look of tenderness in his eyes.

Mrs. Manual came hobbling to the door in spite of her arthritis. "What in the world is going on?" she asked, surprised at the strange procession. "Why is Lori wrapped in that blanket? Well, never mind now, you can tell me later. I'm very glad to see you safe after the fright you gave us all, but we must get you into some dry clothes. Come on into Jo's room and we'll find everything we need."

Soon Lori was dressed in one of Jo's flannel nightgowns. "This feels so warm," she said to Aunt Maud. "It's almost as though Jo herself were here to welcome me. Let me tell you, Aunt Maud, how foolish I have been."

"Lori, you do not need to talk right now. You can tell Uncle Charlie and me later what happened. Come help me, Mrs. Mueller, and we'll all have something to eat and some warm cocoa."

Mama helped Lori get into bed. "How you feel?" she asked in a very concerned voice. "You be tired to your death. Are you still cold?"

"I'm much better now, Mama. Now that I am with you and Papa again everything is wonderful. I have never been so scared in my whole life, Mama. I really thought I would die there by the side of the road and never be able to tell you how sorry I was for what I had done. I only hope you and Papa can forgive me. I was going to find Jo, in Vancouver."

"No more now, my Lori. I now get you something to eat." Soon she arrived with a sandwich and some steaming hot cocoa for Lori, who accepted it gratefully. How good it tasted. The hot cocoa warmed her through and through.

After she had eaten her eyes kept falling shut of their own accord. "I think she's all tuckered out." Mr. Manual said to Mrs. Mueller. "Say good night to your daughter and then come into the living room where we can visit."

Mama smiled, tucked the blankets around Lori, and said, "Let us thank our God before you go to sleep that he brought you safe home to us. And call goodnight to your Papa in the living room."

Lori called goodnight to her Papa and folded her hands to pray, but before she could utter one word she was fast asleep.

Fifteen

When Lori awoke she looked around her trying to figure out where she was. She heard Mama's voice saying, "And how is my girl this morning? Feel better, I hope."

As yesterday's happenings gradually came back to her she realized how lucky she was to be here on this cot in the Manual's spare room. "I don't know, Mama, I feel very thankful, but am still very very tired. Everything seems to ache."

"How about some breakfast?" said Mr. Manual, entering the bedroom with a tray of milk, hot cereal, and toast. "There's nothing like some good food to help you get your strength back, Brown Eyes."

"What time is it?" Lori asked. "I should be getting ready to go to school, but I am still so tired!"

"Don't you worry about that," Mr. Manual said in a consoling voice. "I asked Harry as he went by here this morning to explain to Miss Kent that your house had been destroyed, and that you would not be at school today. I did not say any more than that, though Harry was full of questions. What you will say to Miss Kent is between you and your teacher, and no one else need know. I have a pretty good idea why all this happened, and hope your father can see what a good girl you really are. I think he'll bend a little in time. One thing is sure, he really loves you. I saw that as we were frantically looking for you. So keep that chin up, little girl. By the way, that Harry Toop has quite a case on you. I could see it all over his face."

"The less said about that the better, Uncle Charlie," Lori answered, smiling at him. "That's another thing my Papa frowns upon, me having a boy for a friend. I think I've caused enough trouble for a while, don't you?"

"I agree, Brown Eyes. We'll tackle that one at a later time. Now eat up and go back to sleep. I'll send your Mama back in here." He winked at Lori and left the room.

"Awake already?" Mama asked as she came back to the room. "Did you sleep good?" She felt Lori's forehead. "Ach, Lorchen, but you feel warm! I think you have catched a cold. Go back to sleep. Sleep helps."

Mama came to sit by Lori's bed. "Papa go over to house. He see what he do about our things," she explained. "He said he look you at noon."

Lori smiled in spite of herself. "I think you mean look in on me, right?" Before Mama could reply she was asleep again.

When next Lori opened her eyes she saw Papa sitting by her cot, a look of tenderness in his eyes. "Do you feel well enough to talk just a little?" he asked his daughter.

"Oh yes, Papa, it is time you and I had a good talk. It has been so long!" Lori looked lovingly at him.

"Well, first of all, you do not have to stay in the house any longer. I realize that I was very harsh in my judgment of you. Of course, you could not anyway because there is no longer a house to stay in!" Lori noticed that old gleam in her Papa's eyes and her heart warmed to him. She took his hand and held it tightly in her own.

"I have been wrong to be so cold to you," Papa continued. "When we came home to change our clothes for the conference we saw that your bicycle was gone. First we thought you had forgotten and come home, then ridden your bicycle back to school when you remembered.

When we did not find you at school we became worried. Miss Kent thought that you didn't want to be at the conference, but would be home before dark. As we talked Miss Kent explained a lot of things. She helped me to see how hard it is for you to grow up in a new country and be so very different from all the others. She told Mama and me that you were a fine and good girl, and that having short hair could never change that." Papa looked earnestly at Lori, and then continued, "In my heart I knew this too, but I was afraid that all the new things around you would turn you away from our God and our ways. I also felt that I was not doing my duty if I was not very strict with you. I should have trusted you and believed in you. I will try to be more understanding. However; I insist that you continue to observe our Mennonite ways. They have worked for many generations before us."

"Oh, Papa, you were doing what you thought was right. I knew that. It only hurt so much that you would not believe me about my hair, and that you thought I was doing poor work at school on purpose. I was just so very upset and hated to see you punish my friend Jo, too, when she was not to blame. But most of all I missed your love." Lori's eyes were misty with tears.

Papa patted her head and said softly, "And I missed you, my Lorchen. When Mama and I were on our way home from the conference the storm began. We arrived home and waited. As the wind and rain increased and we still didn't know where you were we were crazy with worry. Even losing our house did not matter. When I saw you I thanked God that He had brought you safely back to us. Lori, you may keep your hair short," Papa continued. "And here is something else."He reached under his chair and pulled out a box. "I found these not harmed in the house. It is all right if you want to wear them." He handed Lori the box with the clothes Aunt Hedwig had sent her.

"Are you certain you would not mind?" Lori asked, a hint of excitement in her voice. "I can be happy now even without them. I want you to know that, Papa."

"It is all right for you to wear them. I will ask, however, that you do not shorten them. I do not want my daughter to show so much of her legs. And if you ever start acting like that Susie Chadsey they go right back in the box, understand?" Papa grinned at her, then said. "I must go now. Mr. Chadsey and Mr. Manual want to talk to me about fixing our house. You continue to rest."

By evening it was obvious that Lori had quite a high fever. Mr. Manual opened the door of her room, saying. "Lori. This is Dr. Patton. We have asked him to look in on you." Mama and Papa entered, looking very worried.

"This girl is suffering from exposure," the Doctor explained after a thorough examination. "You were wise to call me so soon. I will give her medication which, I hope, will prevent complications. It will be necessary for you to miss a week of school, young lady," he said to Lori. "You may get out of bed in a few days if you feel better, and in a week you should be as good as new. Just don't get caught in any more windstorms."

Mama tucked Lori in for the night, kissed her, and left the room with the others.

Just before Lori fell asleep she folded her hands and said fervently, "I thank Thee, God, for making everything all right again. But most of all, I thank Thee for my parents."

Several days passed during which Lori slept a great deal of the time. By Sunday she felt much better, and actually joined the Manuals and her parents for breakfast. Just before lunch there was a knock at the door, and when Mrs. Manual opened it Susie came walking in. "Since it is Sunday I thought I would come check on you. All the kids say hello," Susie informed Lori, "especially Alice and Harry. He says to tell you the project is all finished and handed in. Everyone wants to know where you were that afternoon you left at recess, and so do I. I know my father found you somewhere but he will not talk about it, except to say you were caught in a windstorm. Where in the world did you go, and why?"

"That is something I would rather not talk about for now. Perhaps in time I can talk about it, but right now I just can't."

"If Lori does not want to talk about her adventure you should not press her," Mrs. Manual quickly came to her defense. "As long as her teacher knows, that's all that matters. And I'm sure Lori will tell her."

"You still may be in trouble at school. Kids get detentions for leaving without permission, you know," Susie continued, ignoring Mrs. Manual. "But since you're teacher's pet nothing like that will probably happen to you. Well, I must go. I'll see you at school. though I don't know what I'll tell the other kids about where you were." Susie got up from her chair and left hurriedly.

"What a snippet that one is!" said Mrs. Manual. "Her parents seem quite nice, how could they have raised such an ill mannered child?"

"They spoil her," Mrs. Mueller said. "She only child. She wrap them around little finger. It be hard for her she not change."

There was another knock at the door, and Mr. Chadsey walked in. "I have some great news for you, Lori," he said excitedly. Your dear Uncle Charlie and I met with some of our neighbors, and they are willing to help you people build a new house. I have signed a note making it possible for your father to borrow money for the lumber, which he will pay back on an installment plan."

"We will have two bedrooms, one just for you, a kitchen and a living room," Papa said happily. "I now know how kind all these people are. I can hardly believe the number of men willing to help. Our new home should be ready in two weeks."

"Oh Papa, how wonderful! Mama will have a real kitchen and I will have my own special room! I will invite everyone at school to see it!" Lori's eyes sparkled with joy. She rose impulsively and hugged everyone at the table.

Later that afternoon Uncle Charlie came in with a big bouquet of yellow roses in his hands." These were sent by Jo to help you get well, along with all her love, and a letter is on the way. She has convinced her parents that she should spend a part of her summer here with us. How's that for good news?"

"That is just wonderful!" Lori hugged her dear friend. "I want you to know, everything is turning out all right after all! I guess it does help to pray to God," she added thoughtfully.

"Maybe it does, dear Brown Eyes. I guess I should give it a try myself," Mr. Manual said, eyes twinkling. "I saw the florist delivering these flowers, and had a hunch they were for you. But now I must get back to work. We have begun the frame on your house, and the sooner it is finished the better for all of you."

The week passed quickly. By Friday Lori was feeling as good as new, and was actually looking forward to school on Monday. She could hardly wait to wear her red plaid skirt and white sweater, with white knee socks to match, even though they would look like stockings with her long skirt. Her thoughts were interrupted by a knock at the door.

"Are you ready for some visitors?" Mrs. Manual asked as she answered it

There stood Miss Kent accompanied by Harry and Alice. "I'm so glad you are well again." Alice said, throwing her arms around Lori.

"That goes for me too." Harry grinned at Lori. "The nerve of you getting sick and leaving me with the science project to finish. Miss Kent and I sent it in, but next year I expect you to work at it until it is completed. Of course you'll have to do it by yourself since I'll be in high school. But with all this excellent practice you should have a good chance to win."

"You two did well enough, considering Lori's emotional state," Miss Kent said. "I'm glad to see you looking well. According to Susie you were quite ill. Perhaps one day you will tell me just what happened the afternoon of your conference."

"I acted very foolishly and tried to run away, Miss Kent. I did not think your talk with my parents would help. I should have stayed, no matter what." Lori spoke with eyes downcast.

"Yes, you should have stayed. Your attempt to run away expressed a lack of confidence in me as well as your parents." Miss Kent said." I had a long talk with them, you know. I hope I was able to smooth some of the rough places. But you must remember that it is as hard for them to adjust to new ways as it is for you to obey them when you are convinced they are wrong. All this takes time. You must have patience with them too."

Tears came to Lori's eyes. "I will try." she said thoughtfully. "I know it will be hard sometimes. I know Papa and I will have other problems. But I will remember what you said about having patience with him too. And I will never again doubt his love for me.

I thank you, Miss Kent, for helping me understand that."

When her three visitors had left Lori went back to the spare room, took a piece of paper from her school notebook, and began to write.

"Dear Diary:

I'm so sorry you were destroyed in the storm. This piece of paper will have to do until I can get a new notebook. So much has happened I hardly know where to begin.

First of all, I will have a real room of my own very soon. Our new house will be finished in a matter of weeks. I can hardly wait.

Papa and I are close once more. He is even going to allow me to wear my new clothes though I may not shorten them. I am sure Papa and I will have other problems. One of them will be Harry. Papa does not approve of boy friends, and I like him so much. But I think he realizes that you can look nice on the outside and not change on the inside except to feel a little better about yourself.

Another will be Susie. I'm sure she will not change her attitude towards me very soon, if ever. But some of the other girls are getting to know me, so maybe Susie won't matter quite as much. And if she does not have her way all the time because the girls are getting to know me, she will have to be less rude.

I want to tell you that I got an arrangement of beautiful yellow roses from Jo as well as a letter telling me that she will be allowed to spend part of her summer here. That is the best gift of all.

I promise you, dear diary, that I will remember to thank God for my blessings, even when things aren't going just as I want them to.

I will begin right now. I thank Thee, God, for my country, for my understanding teacher, for my new home, and for my friends.

But most of all, I thank Thee for my parents.

Printed in the United States
93470LV00001B/88-135/A